HOPEFULLY MATCHED

CATHRYN BROWN

Sienna Bay Press

PO Box 158582

Nashville, Tennessee 37215

www.cathrynbrown.com

Cover designed by Najla Qamber Designs

(www.najlaqamberdesigns.com)

Publisher's Note: This is a work of fiction. Names, characters, places, and incidents are a product of the author's imagination. Locales and public names are sometimes used for atmospheric purposes. Any resemblance to actual people, living or dead, or to businesses, companies, events, or institutions is completely coincidental.

Hopefully Matched/Cathryn Brown. - 1st ed.

ISBN: 978-1-945527-37-1

❀ Created with Vellum

DEAR READER

I'm happy to share this story with you. It takes place in Homer, Alaska, one of my favorite places on Earth. When I was a child, my family often made the five-hour drive from Anchorage to spend a weekend in this tiny town beside Kachemak Bay.

Aimee spent happy times here when she was growing up. Jack is from another part of the state and found Homer as an adult.

Aimee owns a jewelry store. Because I grew up in a family jewelry business, and later became a writer for a major jewelry publication, I'm an expert in it. I sprinkled in some extra little facts that you might not know about jewelry.

I hope you enjoy this third book in the series. The matchmakers are working to make this match a success

CHAPTER ONE

"Bro, I have a big favor to ask of you," Adam said. Jack set down his camera so he could give his full attention to his older brother. Adam didn't ask for too many favors.

"By the way, just yesterday someone mentioned what great wedding photos we had and asked for our photographer's contact information." Adam chuckled.

Jack grinned. "I hope you didn't give him my number. Not that I don't love you, bro, but I'm glad that your wedding with Holly was my one and only wedding shoot. I was happy to do it for you two, but I'm going to stick with nature photography."

"No problem. I'm not calling about photos." Adam paused, and that made Jack wonder what was going on. "Now that I think about it, though, I suspect you're going to have to take photos whenever our other brothers get married. That's three more, since you can't do your own."

"I'm not planning to get married for a long time, so that isn't likely to be a problem."

It seemed like Adam started to say something and then changed his mind. "I called today because Mark is going to propose to Maddie soon. I stopped by yesterday and had coffee with him. He has barely left her side, but he stepped away from her long enough to do that."

"I've always thought they belonged together. That's awesome!"

Adam laughed. "I worried that he just felt guilty for more or less causing her current problems. I didn't want him to stay with her because of guilt. But he clearly loves Maddie and seems to be his old, happy self."

Another long silence caused Jack to shift on his feet.

"He wants to buy her a ring."

Jack shrugged. "That makes sense. But what does that have to do with me?"

"At a family dinner last night, I mentioned it, and my sister-in-law Bree had a great idea. She and Michael love Homer and are considering buying a vacation home there. In a romantic voice, she explained that she fell in love with Homer when she was falling in love with Michael. That sounds just a bit too girly for me."

Jack laughed. "You're right on that. But I agree that Homer is a great place to live. I'm still in a short-term apartment rental, but I'm searching for a place to live here. It's just over an hour's drive to Mom and Dad, so close—"

"But not too close." Adam laughed.

"I am confused about this call, though. Bree had an idea because she likes Homer. I live in Homer. Do you want me to do something here?"

Adam sighed. "The idea grew. Holly, Bree, and Jemma came up with a plan, and Holly brought it to me. Other than ordering something online, which none of them seem to be in favor of, this seemed like the best idea."

Jack shifted on his feet. "Spit it out, brother. What do the girls want me to do? It's a gorgeous day, and I'm about to take some photos that I hope do the light justice."

"They want you to go to a jewelry store in Homer. Bree has stopped in a few times—she apparently likes jewelry—and has gotten to know the owner."

Jack had tried to sell his own jewelry store outside of Fairbanks for over a year, and when he had, he'd said he wouldn't set foot in another one for a long time. As he started sputtering and prepared objections, Adam continued. "You just have to go in and snap some photos of rings you think Maddie would like, send those to Mark, and he'll choose the ring."

"That's easy." Other than the part where he had to be in a jewelry store, but he wasn't going to mention that. He helped family when he could. "Is there a catch, or is this as simple as it sounds?"

"None that I know of. But I should warn you that Holly and her sisters are giddy from matchmaking success right now. Holly helped Noah and Rachel get together, and Jemma played matchmaker with Mark and Maddie."

A rush of panic surged through Jack. "That only leaves Bree, and she must want to be a matchmaker too. Are you saying—"

Adam interrupted. "I'm as sure as I can be that they just want you to scout out rings." Jack could hear hesitation in his brother's voice.

"There's no sense in drawing out the dread I'm feeling." Jack tucked his camera back into his camera bag. "I'm on my way now."

3

When they'd ended the call with a promise that both Jack and Adam would be at his parents' house for Saturday lunch, he looked wistfully at the scene in front of him. Kachemak Bay spread out before him with the Homer Spit, a giant gravel bar stretching into the water, and mountains framing the opposite side of the bay. Even though it was an overcast day, one of many he'd seen here, this view never failed to light his imagination.

At that moment, the clouds parted, and rays of sunlight beamed through the hole in the clouds. Jack grabbed his camera and started snapping photos. As quickly as it had appeared, it disappeared. But he'd caught it.

After putting away his gear, he headed into town.

Aimee stepped out of the back room when she heard the bell over the door chime. One of her favorite people came through the door.

"Mrs. Sims! It's always a pleasure to see you. Are you in Homer for the weekend with your husband again?"

Mrs. Sims grinned. "Retirement is a beautiful thing. This time we're here for the whole week. I told him that I needed to stop by one of my favorite stores to see what's new."

Aimee smiled. "And you meant my shop, not Cinnamon Bakery, right?"

Her customer laughed. "I will admit to being interested in anything they make over there. In my opinion, they'd be hard-pressed to do any better than that cinnamon roll. But I meant your store, yes."

Aimee's mouth started watering at the thought of eating one of those sweet treats. As she walked toward the glass case that held her custom pieces, Mrs. Sims followed her. Aimee reached into the case and brought out a pair of morganite earrings she thought her customer might enjoy. The woman's eyes lit up as soon as she saw the square pink stones, each surrounded by a frame of tiny white-gold beads.

"Did you make these earrings?"

Satisfaction rolled through Aimee. "I did."

Mrs. Sims stepped in front of the mirror on the counter, picked up the earrings, and held them next to her ears. "These are dreamy, Aimee. What was your inspiration for them?"

"I bought the stones at the Tucson Gem Show in Arizona last February. I was still looking for a jewelry store to buy or a place to start one from scratch, so buying the stones was silly, but they were so pretty that I bought them anyway."

"And the inspiration?"

"As I sat having a cup of coffee on the deck while the sun rose one morning, a whale crested the water in the bay. The frothy water with the pink sky inspired these earrings and a necklace."

Mrs. Sims gave her a sideways glance. "A necklace? Has someone bought it yet?"

"I put the set in the case only yesterday." Aimee brought the necklace out and laid it beside the earrings.

Her customer tried on the necklace. Staring in the countertop mirror, she said, "Sold!"

Aimee struggled to hide her glee. Not only did her customer want her labor-of-love jewelry, but she would pay enough for the set to keep her going for a while as she settled into her still-new business. She wanted to grin like a fool. But being a professional, she stayed calm, boxed up the jewelry, completed the transaction, handed Mrs. Jones the bag, and waved to her as she left with a smile.

Standing patiently at the counter, she waited until her customer stepped beyond the store's front windows, then spun in a circle with her arms outstretched. "Whee! She loved them!" Moving to Homer *had* been the right thing to do.

When she came to a stop, she found a man standing half inside, half outside the glass front door and staring at her like she'd lost her mind.

The problem with shouting for glee was that one couldn't always hear the bell chime.

The man, of course, a handsome man she'd never met, continued to stare at her as if he expected her to do something else strange.

"Um, welcome to Homer Gems."

He took a few steps inside, then stopped and glanced around the store and over his shoulder as though he was looking to see if anyone else was around. He made her just a tiny bit nervous, and not for the first time, she wondered if she should hire an employee. Of course, employees wanted to be paid consistently, and her business wasn't there yet.

He continued toward her and cleared his throat. "I'd like to look at engagement rings."

Aimee hid a smile behind her hand. She doubted he had any criminal tendencies. His nervousness was purely because he, an unwed man, wanted to look at wedding rings. She directed him to the other side of the store to the chairs in front of the bridal jewelry case and gestured for him to sit down.

"I'm Aimee Jones."

He put out his hand. "Jack O'Connell. And I should tell you that Bree Kinkaid sent me."

Aimee grinned. "Bree's great! Both as a customer and as a doctor. I had a splinter one day, and she helped me." When she said *splinter*, he got a puzzled expression, so she explained. "I was building shelves in the back." She pointed toward the doorway that led to what she lovingly called her studio.

Turning back to her customer, she asked, "Do you know what you're looking for?"

He shook his head and gulped. "It's probably best if I explain her personality and how she dresses in the hope that you can pull together a few rings she might enjoy. Then I'll take photos of them and send them off."

Well, at least he hadn't just ordered online. If he wanted to send photos to his intended and not have the woman come in to look herself, she could work with him. "Why don't you describe her appearance first."

"She has shoulder-length blonde hair, and her eyes are . . . blue." He nodded his head. "Yes, her eyes are blue."

He looked up at her as if asking for her to give him the next question. She suspected he would be a less than observant husband if he wasn't certain of the eye color of the woman he planned to marry.

"You're sure they're blue?"

He closed his eyes. When he opened them, he said, "I can picture her now. Her eyes are the color of the sky over Kachemak Bay on a sunny day."

Aimee's eyes widened. The man must be a poet. Or a painter.

"Do we have a budget to be respectful of?"

"Yes." He told her the figure he'd been given.

"And her fashion style?"

"She seems to love jeans but also wears business suits to work every day. She rarely wears jewelry beyond simple earrings. Does any of that help?"

Based on what he'd said, Aimee considered the rings in the case, deciding on three to show him. "Have you noticed if she wears clothes that are more feminine or more outdoorsy —for lack of a better word?"

He looked into her eyes and hesitated for just a second. Pulling his gaze from hers, he said, "She isn't very girly. No ruffles or frilly things. In her home, she seems to prefer colors from nature. Her house is being decorated in blues and greens."

Aimee changed her mind about one of the rings, swapping out one with diamonds in a floral pattern for another with cleaner lines. She reached into the jewelry case in front of her and pulled out the three engagement and wedding ring sets on stands and put them in front of him.

Jack studied the rings, taking each off the stand and turning it in the light. Then he took out his phone and snapped photos of the rings from different angles. As he stood, he said, "We'll get back to you with the choice very quickly. I'll text you the answer."

She handed him her business card. He entered her number in his phone, sent her a text message, and she added him to her contacts. As he turned to leave, she reached out her hand and touched his elbow. "We'll also need to know her ring size, or she can come to the store after she receives the ring."

Jack rolled his eyes. "I should have thought of that. We'll figure it out. This is going to be a surprise."

"Oh, so the fiancée-to-be isn't going to see the photos?"

"No, just my brothers and assorted other family, probably including Bree." He looked back to the rings. "My pick is this one." He pointed to the ring on the far right.

She smiled and tried to keep her manner professional, not too excited. "That's one I designed and made."

"You're a jewelry designer?"

She nodded. "I am. I can make pretty much anything you can think of. I enjoy the challenge. I take the precious metal, then I shape and polish it until it becomes something beautiful." She realized she'd gushed. "At least it's beautiful to me."

He looked at that ring again. "It's beautiful to everyone. You do wonderful work." Then he waved and left the store.

Aimee's heart went pitter-patter, and she sighed. Too bad the man was about to be engaged.

CHAPTER TWO

*A*s soon as Jack left the jewelry store, he sent the photos to Mark and Adam. Then he went toward the bakery where he'd have a place to sit while he went over his next steps.

After placing his order for a cup of black coffee, he sat and scrolled through rental ads on his phone, trying to find his new home in Homer. Frustrated within a few minutes, he sighed and set his phone down. His order arrived, and fortified by a cup of some of the best coffee he'd ever had, he pondered his situation.

Every day in a hotel, even an inexpensive hotel, cost him a lot more than he wanted to pay a month. He'd been planning to be a photographer for a while, had saved for it, and made a profit from the sale of his business, but that didn't mean he wanted to throw his money into the wind and have it blow away. He wanted to be frugal as he grew his business.

The waitress stopped and asked if he'd like a refill just as he picked up his phone and started browsing through ads again.

"I'm not trying to be nosy, but are you looking for a place to live?"

He looked up at her and smiled. She was old enough to be his mother, so he suspected she was just small-town nice. "I am. Do you know of anything?"

"Do you need a home for the long-term or just for a short time?"

Jack cocked his head to the side. "Eventually long-term, because I am planning to live in Homer, but right now, I'd be happy to have something that was day-by-day until I found that place."

She smiled. "Then I may have the right thing for you. We rent it out by the day during the summer, but tourist season is wrapping up for the year, so we can give you a great deal on a week-to-week rental."

"You have my interest."

She went over to the cashier station, where she wrote something down. She brought back a piece of paper with an address and a phone number on it. "Drive by and see if you're interested. If you are, I'll meet you there after work and show you the place. I can't promise to answer the phone if you call because I'm a potter and often get lost in my work. This is my daughter's bakery, though, so you can find me through her if you ever need to."

Jack smiled at her, enjoying small-town friendliness. "I'll look at it. Thank you." He didn't mention that he wasn't holding his breath on this one. Every place he'd looked at had been wrong on too many levels. As he started his life over away from his jewelry business, he knew he wanted to have a home that had natural beauty, a place where he could wake up, step outside, and take a photo of something gorgeous. He took the piece of paper from her and thanked her, promising to let her know either way later in the day.

After a coffee refill and the purchase of a blueberry muffin for a snack later, he went back to his vehicle and drove to the address. When he stopped in the driveway, he stared slack-jawed at a gorgeous view of Kachemak Bay. Without hesitating, he sent a text to his future temporary landlord and said he'd like to meet her there later. The money she'd quoted him was much less than a hotel. It might not work long-term, but for this view and that price, he didn't care too much about the interior. This was definitely a step in the right direction.

Aimee entered her jewelry store and locked the door behind her. Then she hurried over to the alarm panel and turned it off. Once she'd stowed her purse in the tiny office space in the back, she retrieved the jewelry she'd put in the safe last night. Her insurance required that the more expensive pieces were stored safely behind a combination lock.

She took out the trays of jewelry for the front display window that passersby would see from the sidewalk. As she carried it to the front of her store, she checked it and decided to stop and clean a couple of the pieces so they would sparkle and catch the light better. It didn't take being handled too many times by potential buyers before the oils on people's hands dulled the stones.

With that done, she put the jewelry into the front window, carefully arranging each piece around what she hoped was a random-looking assortment of imitation fall leaves she'd bought inexpensively. Many of them were for trees that didn't even grow here, but they looked pretty and set the tone for the season, and that was all she cared about.

She put the jewelry from the safe where it belonged in the rest of the cases, grateful that she didn't have to put everything in there. Only the more expensive and vulnerable pieces such as those in the front window and the diamond rings went into it nightly.

A knock on the door had her looking up. Her friend Molly, the owner of Cinnamon Bakery up the street, waved at her from outside. Aimee hurried over and unlocked the door, locking it behind herself because she still had a half hour before opening.

"What are you doing here, Molly? Isn't it your morning rush right now?"

Molly's eyes lit up. "I had to tell you about the man that I just met."

Aimee fought against rolling her eyes and lost the battle. "Another new guy?"

Molly shrugged. "At least I get out there. When was the last time you went on a date?"

When was the last time that she had done *anything* that didn't involve work? She stayed silent, hoping that would cause her friend to move on to another topic. It didn't. Aimee finally broke the silence. "You know what it's like to start a business. I know yours has been open over two years, so the growing pains and newness aren't as intense as they are here. Every waking hour and every thought has to do with Homer Gems."

Molly reached out her hand and put it on Aimee's arm. "I know that the business is important to you, but you've got to come up for air. You have to do something that's fun."

Molly's words rang true in Aimee's head, but that didn't

change her situation. She pressed her fingers against her forehead and thought about the week ahead. If she rearranged her Thursday, she could go out with her grandfather on one of his boats. She always quieted down when she was on the saltwater. "To make you happy, I'll tell Grandpa that I'll go with him on Thursday for one of his halibut charters."

Molly shook her head. "I was thinking *fun* as in get your nails done, have lunch with a friend, smile at a handsome man."

Aimee laughed. The image of Jack standing in her open door staring at her while she waved her hands around with glee came to mind. "I met a handsome man in here yesterday. But I think I scared him off." At Molly's puzzled expression, she explained what happened.

"He was probably just a visitor to Homer, so you're safe. I doubt you'll ever see him again."

Aimee thought over what he'd told her. "You may be right. One of my good customers sent him in. He's her sister's brother-in-law. He was in town and needed to buy an engagement ring."

Molly's eyebrows raised. "You're talking about an engaged man? I thought you meant someone who was available." She waved her hand in front of her face. "Don't sweat that. At least you *thought* he was handsome. That's something anyway."

Aimee giggled. Her phone pinged, so she reached over and picked it up. She'd received a text from Jack O'Connell. "The man we were speaking of just sent me a message."

Family agrees on the wedding engagement ring set that you made.

She turned the phone to face Molly and gave her friend a

wide grin. "I enjoy making my buyers happy, but it makes me extra happy when they buy jewelry that *I* made."

"There's a parallel in my business. If I sold a customer a cookie someone else had made, that would be okay. But when they buy something that I made or at least was made in my bakery, it makes me happy. When they tell me they loved it, that's even better and does something special to me inside."

Another message followed with an address and payment details. "Exactly. I just need to box up the set and send it to this address in Anchorage. Jack says that he will be—no, his brother will be—calling with a credit card number." She looked up at Molly. "Don't you think it's strange that someone other than the groom is going to be calling with payment information?"

Molly shrugged. "Maybe his family is loaning him money to buy the ring set. I'm sure a lot of people must buy something like that with a credit card or with some sort of payment system. It would probably be better if it was family instead of a stranger loaning the money. I did notice that you're on a first-name basis with your customer."

Aimee replied. "He called me Aimee from the moment we met, probably because that's how my customer spoke of me. So I called him Jack." She set her phone down. "Well, no matter who's paying, I just started my day out very nicely." Her phone pinged again, and she picked it up. "I'm sorry about being rude like this, Molly."

Her friend said, "Business is business."

"This is also mysteriously written. It says the bride- and groom-to-be will come into the store to resize the ring if that's needed."

Molly turned the lock on the door and pulled it open. "I'd

better get back to work. Everything's baked, and there was just a little bit of a lull, so I thought I'd run over." As she started to leave, she added, "And don't forget my advice. I was distracted temporarily by your handsome customer story. You'll have to take a break from work and come for a cup of coffee to hear my story."

"No fair! I shouldn't leave the store."

"Put up that clock sign and tell your customers you'll be back in a half hour. In case I don't see you again today—" Molly gave Aimee a mock glare "—I'm telling you now that you need to do something other than business. And I'm not sure that spending the day helping on a halibut fishing charter is the answer." She stepped out, and the door closed behind her before Aimee could come up with a good response.

Maybe Molly was right, and she did need to find time to do something other than business.

Jack rented the studio apartment and happily woke up the next morning to an amazing view of dawn over the bay. Now, if he could just find a place to live permanently with a view that was even half as good as this, then his move to Homer would be a success.

When he'd owned his jewelry store, Saturday morning would have meant he'd already worked five days and had to finish his sixth, the last one before his only day off. He would take photos early in the morning, evenings, and Sunday afternoon. He'd rejoiced when snow had closed roads on a couple of weekdays, so he could close the store and take photos of the new snowfall.

Today, he could spend an hour snapping photos of whatever he wanted to. Later, when the light wasn't as good, he would tweak some of them in a photo editing program and upload those to a site for sale.

He fixed oatmeal and stood on his small deck to eat it and watch seagulls sailing on the wind. With his hot cereal half eaten and thoughts of a smoothie on his mind, his phone rang.

Adam again. It wasn't that they didn't talk often, but he didn't usually call first thing in the morning. Especially not now that he had a wife and the twin girls he had officially adopted last week.

"Jack, Holly, and her sisters have come to me with another idea. Before I tell you about it, can you describe the owner of Homer Gems?"

A cold chill settled over Jack. "She's pretty and probably in her late twenties. She was dressed in very girly clothes, for lack of a better description. Pink. Lace. Her hair is somewhere between the colors of blonde and brown, about halfway down her back and pulled back."

"Is she pretty? I should say . . . was she pretty to *you?*"

Jack groaned. "She would be pretty to anyone. Adam, have I been set up?"

Silence greeted him.

"The matchmakers *are* at it again?"

"I'm starting to think that's a very strong possibility. I haven't confronted Holly about it yet. I wanted to talk to you first. If she'd been Mom's age, I would have known I was wrong."

Jack thought back over the experience when he'd been in the store. Aimee had been professional, at least she'd been professional after she'd stopped twirling. "I don't believe she

17

thought about me in that way. It's a small town, so I probably will run into her again now and again, but I shouldn't need to say more than a few words to her. I think I'm safe from your wife and her sisters."

Another period of silence greeted him. "Before you get too confident, remember that I mentioned a new plan when I called. And I personally know that when those three sisters get together, you never know what's going to happen."

Jack chuckled. "They do seem to be a force to be reckoned with."

"So true. Anyway, Mom's birthday is in a few months. For some reason, it never occurred to us to give her this when you owned your jewelry store, and I don't know why. They suggested a necklace that had the birthstones for each of her five boys."

Jack thought over the idea. He didn't usually like birthstone jewelry because of the crazy combinations of colors that often resulted, so it hadn't occurred to him. This would be different. "I actually think that's a genius idea. Mom would love it. And if it had some sort of flower pattern that the stones were set in or around, it would be one of her favorite gifts ever. But what does this have to do with me?"

When Adam didn't immediately answer, he knew why. Jack slowly said, "I need to go back to Homer Gems, don't I?"

He could picture his older brother grinning when he said, "That's the plan. Unless you know of a jewelry designer who could do a better job. Bree seems to think a lot of this woman."

The work that Jack had seen in the store was first-rate. Her jewelry-making skills far exceeded his own. Aimee Jones took it to an art form.

"Are you there?"

"I am." There was only one answer to his brother's earlier question. "This jeweler will do a fabulous job for Mom. I'll go see her. But I'm going to keep my guard up. It isn't that I don't ever want to get married, but I just found my freedom after selling the jewelry store. For years, I was trapped there day after day after day, and the last thing I want to do is to be connected to anyone who is going to tie me down. To be connected to someone who owns a jewelry store . . ." He shuddered. "The girls have completely missed it on this one, and I may have to let them know next time I see them."

"My guess is that this was Bree's idea. But I think they're all in on it together."

"Andy isn't safe then, is he?"

Adam chuckled. "Probably not. I wonder if I should warn him or just let things roll along."

Jack thought about his brothers. Adam, Noah, and Mark were all amazingly happy, one of them married and two to be married soon. "Why don't you just let it lie? If they come up with someone who Andy falls in love with, that's great. I'll take care of everything we need to do to create this piece of jewelry for Mom. I'm going to keep it professional with one visit to order and maybe another for follow-up. Otherwise, I'm going to stay as far away from this woman as I can."

"You are in control, Jack. They can only invite you to have a match made. It's just that they've been very good at it thus far."

With that, they ended the call.

CHAPTER THREE

*I*t seemed like the matchmakers had put a target on his chest, but instead of a circular bull's-eye, there was a heart in the middle, and they were playing Cupid by shooting arrows into him. Jack stepped out onto the tiny front porch of the cottage he'd rented and stared out at the view before him. Taking a sip of coffee, he pondered the situation.

He wanted to call Adam and tell him "No," that he would not go to the jewelry store, but they'd had a great idea. Every year, the five brothers struggled with ideas for something to give their mother for her birthday. Bree and her sisters had come up with something that she would love. While he could send someone else to do it, of all the people in the family, he alone had the experience to get the job done right, and he wasn't going to disappoint them.

He marched inside, set his cup of coffee down on the counter, and went out, locking the door behind him. No matchmaker was going to keep him away from the duties that his family had assigned to him.

About a half hour later, Jack stopped in front of the jewelry store's display window and looked in the window to see if Aimee Jones was doing anything odd again before he entered. She handed a customer a small paper bag and smiled broadly at them. The customer came out of the door, and he heard the bell ding. She picked up a bottle of spray cleaner, sprayed the glass countertop in front of her, and began wiping it. Aimee seemed perfectly normal. He entered the store, and her expression was first one of recognition and then of anxiousness.

"Is something wrong with the rings? Maddie—isn't that what you said her name was?—hasn't come in to get them fitted yet."

"She's healing from a fall, but I'm sure she'll be in in a few weeks. I'm here for something completely different. Bree Kincaid and her sisters came up with what I have to admit is a wonderful idea for my mother's birthday. All five of us brothers are going to chip in for it, and we want you to make it."

"Okay. I'm happy to do what I can. What is this idea?"

"We're going to do our birthstones in a necklace."

When she fought against a grimace, he chuckled. "I know those can be really ugly because the combinations of colors don't always go together. In this case, we were born in months that make this work very well, but the gemstones are also more on the expensive side."

"I once had to make a necklace with a yellow-green peridot next to a red ruby next to a pearl and with a large blue topaz for the mother herself." She shuddered. "I know that there's love behind it, and the recipient was thrilled, but it doesn't fit my design aesthetic."

"Well, the five boys' birthstones include one diamond for

April, two sapphires for September, and two garnets for January." He told her the amount of money they wanted to spend.

She nodded as she made notes on a pad she'd grabbed from a side counter. "That's nice. We'll have the clear diamond, blue sapphires, and I can choose garnets to add the right pop of color since they come in so many variations across a broad spectrum. Hmm." She tapped her pencil on her check. "The deep pink-violet color of rhodolite garnet might be nice."

He grimaced, and she laughed.

"It is for Mom, and you're absolutely right that she would appreciate the pink much more than I would."

Aimee smiled broadly, and it caught Jack off guard. She went from pretty to beautiful in a pink, feminine way. He'd been so focused on his task at hand that he hadn't taken time to look at her today—probably out of self-preservation against matchmaking—but he did now. She had on a bright pink top with a lace vest and a long skirt with the same pink and some other colors. Not everyone could wear it well, but she carried it off with aplomb.

She stared down at the list and flipped the pencil from side to side between her thumb and forefinger. "I'm running through design ideas—"

He interrupted her. "It needs to have a flower or some sort of floral pattern."

She looked up at him with a questioning expression on her face.

"Our mother is famous for the flowers that she wears. One might be embroidered on her purse or printed on a shirt or down the leg of her pants, but it's a rare day when she isn't wearing something—if not many things—with flowers. It even extends to her shoes."

"Her style sounds . . . interesting." She seemed to be fighting a smile at the description of the would-be necklace wearer's personal style.

Jack laughed. "Mom knows it's over the top, but she has five sons and a husband, so she spent decades without another woman in the house. And Dad only lets her carry flowers into the house in small ways. At this point, that's the guest room." He shuddered. "All of us dread nights that we've been in Kenai and have had to sleep in that room."

Still smiling, Aimee looked down at the piece of paper and started to sketch a flower. "Does it have to be realistic, or can I make it more free-form and artistic?" She continued sketching, testing one design, and then moving on to another.

"As long as it's pretty and looks like a flower, I think you will make my mother very happy."

She gave him a small nod as she continued working. She chewed on her upper lip and flipped to a fresh piece of paper, sketching more quickly. He watched the design emerge in front of his eyes and could see the talent this woman had.

When she finished, she turned the paper toward him and stood watching him with obvious trepidation.

A bouquet of flowers with a gemstone the bud of each hung from a chain. "It's perfect! You can do this in our budget?"

"Yes. It's actually fairly lightweight because I've tried to minimize the amount of metal to compensate for the fact that your mother gave birth to sons in the more expensive months of April and September."

He laughed. "That was nervy of her, wasn't it?"

They stared at each other for a moment, then both glanced away. Whew! He'd felt an unexpected zing of attraction. Had she felt it too?

She cleared her throat and said, "Do you need to ask your brothers for approval, or should I begin working on this?"

He had a hard time focusing on her question. She would be all wrong for him in *so many ways*. Aimee not only had a jewelry store, she also seemed ultra girly, and he wanted someone more outdoorsy to be at his side as he traveled. He needed to keep his wits about him.

Focus, Jack. Focus. "I'll text all of them." He pulled his phone out of his pocket and snapped a photo of her sketch, sending it off to all four brothers at once. Replies came back immediately from Mark and Andy.

Noah took a few minutes more to reply and commented, *You caught me as I was boarding the plane. Mom will love it!*

Finally, Adam replied. *Just got out of class. It's perfect. How are you faring with Bree's match for you?*

He nervously glanced over at Aimee then realized she couldn't see what was on his phone. He fired off a reply. *She's not my match.* Then he turned back to Aimee. "They all love it."

Aimee stood proudly and beamed. "That's such a relief. It's my art form, and each design is from my heart. I wonder every time if the customer will like what I created for them"

She went back to that same side counter and returned with a computer tablet, which she scrolled through. "When do you need this?"

"Her birthday is in the second week of November. Could you have it done by the first of the month?"

"That's perfect. Do I need to allow time for shipping it somewhere as I did with the rings?"

"No. I've moved to Homer. I will pick it up when it's ready and will make a point to be in town." *If* he managed to find a more permanent place to live by then.

She made her notes on her device, and he gave her a deposit. With the transaction over, they both awkwardly stood there for a moment before Jack realized he needed to go. "I'll see you then."

She gave a faint smile. "Yes, I'll see you."

Even though he knew better, that he should leave, he wanted to open the door to seeing her again. "I know what it's like to be in a business, and you can't get away for lunch. Can I go pick something up for you and bring it back? I could get enough for the two of us and keep you company." What on earth had made him say the last part? His mouth had gotten ahead of his head.

Aimee tensed up and, in a very proper voice, said, "No, thank you. I'll be fine. I'll let you know if I have any more questions about the project."

He glanced once at her stone-faced expression, turned, and headed for the door. He wasn't sure what he'd said wrong, but it had clearly been something.

Jack walked away slowly and then picked up speed, walking faster and faster as he went away from Homer Gems. What had he been thinking when he'd made that offer? He would normally want to check in often on a project of this nature to make sure it was progressing according to the specifications, but Aimee Jones was a master at what she did. He was certain that whatever the result, his mother would be thrilled with it. Aimee had a feminine sensibility that he thought his mother would appreciate. He could leave Aimee alone.

Now, he just needed to get back to work without any distractions. There were only two things he had to do the rest of this week. One was that he needed to take some great photos he could sell. Nothing brought him more joy than taking photos. The second thing was that he needed to go to lunch at his parents' house on Saturday. He'd missed far too many of those when he'd lived hours away in Fairbanks.

Aimee paced back and forth behind the counters of her jewelry store. What kind of jerk would buy a wedding ring set, propose to a woman who was apparently recovering from some sort of injury, and then come in and offer to have lunch with another woman? And it hadn't seemed like a business lunch either. There had been a personal note to his words and his expression.

She checked her watch, one her grandmother had given her. The same woman she seemed to have inherited her love of all things pretty and girly from. It was just 11:00 a.m., but she could have an early lunch up at Molly's bakery. A cruise ship was docking in Homer this afternoon and should bring business to her store, so she definitely wanted to be available then.

She reached under the counter and pulled out her *Be Right Back* sign with the clock on it, adjusted it to forty-five minutes from now, hung it on the door with a little suction cup, and went out, locking the door behind herself. She didn't bother with the alarm during the day because it was a fairly well-trafficked area, at least as far as that went in a small town.

With each step, she gained momentum. The next time she saw Jack—and she knew she would when she'd finished the job, if not before—she might not be able to be as kind, and that could ruin her relationship with Bree, a woman she both liked and considered to be one of her best customers. She hoped Molly had time to visit with her for a second because she needed a friend to talk her down off of this ledge. Aimee pushed open the door to the bakery and found it mostly empty, not a surprise at this too-late-for-breakfast-and-right-at-the-edge-of-lunch hour.

Molly looked up from where she was behind the counter putting some baked goods in a case. Her friend started to smile at Aimee then took a step backward. She reached for her pot of coffee and poured a cup. By the time Aimee had found a seat at a small table in the corner, Molly had arrived with the coffee and was pulling out the chair across from her.

"Has something happened to your grandfather?"

"No. This has nothing to do with anyone not being well. It's that customer I told you about before; remember the handsome one with the engagement set?"

Molly shrugged. "If his fiancée doesn't like the rings, can't she just choose something else from your store? It wouldn't be a loss for you then."

Aimee looked up and strived to compose herself. Looking across at her friend, she said, "I think he might have hit on me today."

"What?" Molly said loudly enough that her few customers turned to look at them.

"Shh. I don't want everyone to know my business."

"Sorry. You're going to have to tell me more than that. Why was he even there? And was this in front of his fiancée?"

Aimee explained about the necklace. Then she told Molly what had happened about the lunch proposal.

"So he was nice to you, and that made you angry?" Molly said the words slowly and carefully like she was trying to sort out what had happened and what on earth had made her friend so upset.

Aimee tried to find the words for her emotions. "I know it sounds silly. But it felt like we connected. I ignored that, because of the, you know, engagement thing, but it didn't seem to stop him."

Molly studied her for a moment. "Drink some coffee, and I'll get you something sweet. That might help put the bad taste of the situation behind you."

A moment later, her friend returned with one of her daily special breakfast muffins. After Aimee had taken a bite of it, she discovered it had chocolate chips and that she did feel a little bit better. "You're right." Then as she thought about Jack, she started to get angry again. "What do I do, though?" She put another piece of muffin in her mouth.

Molly shrugged. "Treat him nicely but in a businesslike way."

Aimee ate the muffin and brushed off her hands. "Did I make too much of this?"

"I've never known you to do that. Like I said, though, Aimee, you need to get out more. Maybe this wouldn't bother you so much if an actual available man had talked to you recently."

Aimee rolled her eyes. "Yes, Mom, I'll listen. Any other advice, as long as you're handing it out?"

Molly raised an eyebrow. "You could hope that the engagement falls through."

Aimee reached out and shoved playfully on Molly's arm. "The last thing I would want is a potential cheater as a mate. No, I think I'll just keep my eyes open. And I have to hope that whoever I might find is okay with a woman who works six days a week."

"Yeah, about that—"

Aimee held up her hand to stop her friend from speaking. "Don't start in on me about that. Grandpa does that almost every day. I want to make jewelry, and I haven't figured out a way to do that without a jewelry store." She checked her watch. "I'd better get back. Are you ready for the cruise ship people?"

"That's today, isn't it?" Molly's eyes grew wide. "We need to hustle and get some things baked in a hurry." Her friend all but ran to the back of her shop.

Smiling, Aimee got up and went back to hers.

Later that afternoon, Bree Kincaid walked into Aimee's store with a tiny baby in a carrier strapped onto her front.

Aimee clapped her hands in front of herself. "Oh, Bree, she's here! Or is that he?"

Bree grinned. "The first boy born in a generation. Aimee Jones, meet Peter Michael Kinkaid. This is his first road trip, so we thought we should come to Homer." She looked down at her baby and gently ran her hand over the top of his head.

A twinge inside reminded Aimee that she wanted to be a mother. Every once in a while, she thought about having children, but she knew that this point in her life was not the time.

Bree hurried over to the chairs in front of the wedding rings case and sat down. "It feels so good to not waddle anymore, but I'm a little tired off and on. I'd love to look at some earrings if you have anything special?"

Aimee thought through the pieces of jewelry that she had. "Is there a particular color that you're looking for?"

Bree frowned. "Not so much a color as a style. I love earrings that have a little bit of a dangle, but from what I have seen with my patients and with my sister's baby, I don't want to have anything hanging down that he can grab onto and pull."

Aimee took out some pairs of earrings and brought them over.

Bree sorted through them, moving some to the left and some to the right. Aimee could tell that the logical doctor sitting in front of her was narrowing down her choices in an efficient manner. "My sister's brother-in-law—that feels so awkward every time I say it. Why can't I just call him my brother-in-law?"

Aimee laughed. Bree had a way of catching her off guard. "I know. It's like that first cousin or second cousin thing. I'm never exactly sure who is what. I often just say 'cousin.'"

Smiling, Bree continued, "Did Jack come in?"

Aimee struggled to keep a smile on her face. "Yes, he did. He bought the wedding rings. I was happy that he and his bride-to-be had chosen the rings I made. Then he returned to place an order for his mother's birthday gift." She didn't add, *And it seemed like he asked me for a date!*

Bree's head jerked up, and she froze with a pair of topaz

earrings in her hand. Her baby closely watched the sparking gems. "What did you say?"

Aimee thought through the words that she had just spoken. "I said that he bought rings and ordered a necklace?"

Bree shook her head as though she was trying to clear it. "Okay. That makes sense. I thought you said something about Jack getting married."

Aimee felt like smacking the side of her head with the palm of her hand to shake some sense into it. What was going on? "I don't understand. I feel like we're having two different conversations. Jack came in, and he took photos of wedding and engagement ring sets for someone named Maddie. He described how she dressed. He described her. He even very poetically described the color of her eyes. Are you telling me he isn't going to marry her after all? Then why did I get the text yesterday that the family had approved the rings? And why didn't he mention that when he came in today?" If Aimee had a nearby chair to sit on, she would have.

Bree laughed, a belly laugh that startled her baby, and he looked up at her with wide eyes. She cupped the side of his head, still laughing. "It's okay, Petey. Mom is just having some fun here." Focusing on Aimee, she said, "The family sent Jack to look at the rings because he's the only one in the family who has a clue when it comes to anything to do with gems and fine metals. His brother Mark is the one getting married."

Aimee giggled. "This all makes so much more sense now. Mark's paying for his own rings, not for his brother's."

Bree laughed. "Most definitely. Mark and Maddie were high school sweethearts who separated for about fifteen years and then just got together again this summer. They are finally getting married, and they're such a cute couple. I only know the O'Connells because my sister Holly is married to Adam, who is Jack and Mark's brother. Jack isn't even dating anyone." Bree gave Aimee what appeared to be a speculative glance as if she seemed to be weighing her as a possible future date for Jack.

When Aimee didn't comment on Jack, Bree thankfully moved on. She carried the topaz earrings over to a small stand mirror on the counter and held the earrings up to her ears. "These are perfect. The square-cut golden stones look great with my hair color. Don't you think?"

"They're beautiful and a perfect stone to go with fall-colored clothes."

Bree said, "Excellent point. I'll take them." She handed them back to Aimee and took out her credit card.

After Aimee had put them in a box and rung up the sale, she walked her customer to the door receiving a promise from Bree that she would return to Homer soon, and they would get together to have a cup of coffee then.

CHAPTER FOUR

*J*ack walked by Homer Gems and paused for a moment to look at the window and checked his watch. Aimee hadn't put the window display in by 10:00 a.m.? As he watched, Aimee raced out of the back with trays in her hands and hurried toward him. He stepped to the right and out of sight. It would be a little weird to look in the window and not come inside if she did see him. Then he continued on his way. Maybe she'd gotten to work late, but based on their brief time together, he doubted that. She could have gotten caught up in a project and forgotten about it. That also seemed unlikely. He was just glad that he didn't have to deal with retail anymore.

He reached his SUV and considered his options for the day. He'd had his coffee and managed to turn down something sweet at Cinnamon's, but while he'd been there, he'd researched the area on his phone. Homer had become his favorite place in Alaska, but he wasn't a Kenai Peninsula expert. Yet. He'd discovered online that the Anchor River should still have silver salmon in it, and he knew from experience that the area had unparalleled views across the water toward a magnificent range of mountains.

He'd put his camera in his trunk. If he made a quick detour back to his temporary home, he could get his fishing gear. A sunny fall day with superb photo ops and catching salmon for his dinner would make this a dream day.

~

"Today has been a nightmare." Aimee clutched a life-giving mug of coffee at Molly's coffee shop and took a sip, closing her eyes as the creamy elixir slid down her throat.

Molly poured herself a cup of coffee, went over to the door to flip the sign to *closed*, and sat down at one of her small tables. "Sit and tell me what happened."

Aimee did as asked. "First, I am so glad you were still open, but *why* were you open?"

Molly chuckled. "Mom asked her knitting club if they wanted to meet here. I figured I may as well stay open. They could have half the shop, and I'd still serve coffee."

"You are such a smart businesswoman."

Molly watched her friend over the top of her mug as she took a sip of her brew. "I've been in business almost three years. I've learned a thing or two. You'll figure it out."

"*If* my business makes it. You know the statistics for new small businesses."

Molly set her mug on the table. "I've never known Aimee Jones to sound like a quitter. Whatever happened can't be worth quitting over."

Aimee closed her eyes. Could she see herself quitting? No. She stared at Molly. "You're right!" Then the reality of her situation slammed into her. "But I may have a bit of a problem."

"What happened? It can't be that bad."

Aimee took a fortifying swig of her coffee. "I think I told you about the commission to make the wedding set." When Molly nodded, she continued. "The couple has a big budget and liked the most detailed pieces of my jewelry. They had a December wedding planned, so I had plenty of time to fabricate their pieces. I designed an over-the-top detailed set. I may sound like I'm bragging, but this will be a stunning wedding and engagement set, and his coordinating wedding band will be beautiful too."

"I've never known you to be a bragger. Did they cancel?"

"Worse." Aimee sighed. "They're eloping."

Molly grinned. "I've always thought eloping would be fun, but my mother wants a big wedding and might never forgive me." Molly's eyes widened. "*When* are they eloping?"

"Saturday."

"Two days from now?" Molly shouted.

"No, the following Saturday."

"That's plenty of time, isn't it?"

Aimee held out her mug for a refill, and her friend got up to do that. "Thank you. If I could work every minute of every day only on these pieces of jewelry, this would be a challenge, but doable. *But* I have a jewelry store and other people who expect me to work on their jobs too." Her volume climbed with every word. "What am I going to do?"

Molly set the mug down in front of her, and Aimee took a long sip.

"Aimee, you're going to get the rings done. I know the task in front of you seems insurmountable at this moment, but I know that somehow you will finish on time."

"Thank you again. I needed to hear that. It *will* be okay. I *will* succeed." Aimee grinned. "I felt much better when I said that." She drank the rest of her coffee, then stood. "I'd better get home. Grandma will have a great dinner waiting for me."

Molly laughed. "I couldn't wait to get away from my parents when I hit my twenties. You seem to enjoy living with your family."

"Being in England for years meant I rarely saw my family. I'm happy to be around them. I imagine it will wear off. When it starts to, I can move into the cabin Grandma and Grandpa fixed up for me."

"That cabin is so cute that I considered trying to talk my way into it, but I like my home too much to want to move."

Molly unlocked the door as Aimee waited. "Remember to get a coffee break every day."

"I'll try." Aimee hugged her friend. "It's good to be back in Homer and around people who care."

Saturday morning, Aimee hurried through her store. The last two days had been a bit of a blur. For what must be the hundredth time, she went back over the design and what she had left to do, wishing she'd designed simpler rings. If only she'd known about the elopement in the beginning.

She'd added so many special details to the ring set that she could have entered it into a major jewelry design competition. The good news is that they would be beautiful when finished, and she was pretty sure the buyers would love them. But that didn't get the job completed any faster. She had a week left.

After opening her safe, Aimee took out the autumn-colored jewelry for the front window display. Before the elopement craziness had started, she'd taken time to carefully choose the right pieces of jewelry in seasonal colors. Rings, necklaces, and earrings in reddish-brown garnets, golden topaz, and turquoise to give it a pop of brightness made a pretty display. She normally set each ring or necklace out carefully and artistically crafted a display to attract the attention of passersby, but today she upended the tray of jewelry, straightened things out so that nothing was lying on its side and walked away. Pretty would have to wait until next week.

Time to get to work.

At her bench, she studied her job. She decided to make all of the beads for the granulation today. If she could ever manage to get ahead, she would do a stockpile of gold beads so that she would be ready for projects like this. Of course, she'd need to have a lot more money to make them because the gold beads were solid gold. Six months into her business, that was probably wishful thinking. She began the first step of cutting gold into tiny pieces.

Jack walked by Homer Gems and paused for a moment to look in the window. Aimee Jones must be in the process of putting in today's window display. The chaotic assembly of jewelry currently in the window wouldn't be anyone's idea of a selling feature. He continued on to Cinnamon's, his new favorite bakery, for a cup of coffee and one of their somewhat addictive cinnamon rolls. After that, he'd be on his way to his parents' house, getting there early enough to visit before lunch.

On his return trip, he stopped again. Nothing had changed. Sure, all of the jewelry was upright but still seemed chaotic. Maybe she had tried a new style of window display, something avant-garde. This wouldn't be his idea of a successful display, but he certainly wasn't a world expert.

Telling himself that he was checking to see if she had questions about his mother's gift, not just to see if she was okay, he went inside. It wasn't any of his business what she did with her business, and a messy window didn't mean she had problems he should help with.

He pushed open the door, one with quite a few finger-prints and smudges on it. Inside, a group of four people, two men and two women, milled about, but there was no Aimee. The people seemed to be tourists, because they each carried a tote bag with a tour company's name.

Aimee came out of the back room and stepped up to help one of the people.

While she took care of her customer, Jack noticed that the glass cases needed to be cleaned. Everything had been spotless when he'd been here in the past, so she must be very busy to have not cleaned it already.

When he stepped around the case to the employees-only side, she looked over at him with a questioning expression. He picked up the spray bottle of glass cleaner and some paper towels, holding them up in the air as he looked at her. She nodded, and he went to work cleaning the tops of all of the cases except for those right next to her and her customer. Then he stepped around to the front and cleaned that side and looked around to see what else he could do. Before he was done, he had taken care of the fingerprints on the front door, both inside and out. It might seem like a small thing that he was doing for her, but he knew it could feel huge to know that those details were under control.

His efforts had apparently made him appear to be an employee because one of the women walked over to him and loudly asked, "I'm looking for something to remind me of my trip here. Do you have anything?"

He glanced over at Aimee, and she shrugged. She was already busy, so he swallowed his distaste at working in retail and decided that he could do this. "Yes, ma'am. Do you have a budget in mind?"

The woman named a figure that he was happy to work with. He stepped around to the back of the case and steered her over to a display he'd noticed with Alaska jade beads. When he took out a strand of small beads and set them on a pad in front of him, the woman exclaimed over them and tried them on. She scurried over to the mirror to see how they looked. "These are perfect. I'll take them." She turned her back to him so he could unfasten the clasp. Holding the beads, he checked around for a box, found one, and wrapped them, taking care of the sale up until the point when he needed to accept payment.

Aimee was showing the man something in another case, so he walked over to her and handed her the tag from the jade jewelry. "Why don't you ring this up, and I'll take care of this gentleman?" She looked up at him and gave a slow nod, then did what he'd said. When he found something for the man and one of the other people to buy, she rang up those sales, and then they said goodbye to the group as they left.

When they were alone, she smiled and hugged him. "Thank you, Jack!" She released him and, blushing bright red, hastily stepped back. "I'm sorry. We barely know each other."

He hadn't minded the feel of her arms around him, but he

did not want to pursue that concept any further. "You're welcome. I guess I'll be on my way now." His sentence almost had a question mark at the end, even though he hadn't intended for it to.

Switching into professionalism, she said, "You entered at a busy moment, and I appreciate your help. But I wasn't able to ask earlier why you'd come today."

Right. His reason for being here, which had nothing to do with seeing if she was okay. "I wanted to find out if you had any questions about Mom's gift."

Her expression of happiness changed to one of worry as she looked toward the back room. "I'm sorry, but I haven't had time to work on it."

His excuse had put pressure on her. He hurried to add, "It's months away. That's not a problem."

As she faced him again, several people stopped outside her store and made gestures to one another that suggested they liked what they saw.

When they turned and started for the door, Aimee groaned then slapped her hand over her mouth. "I'm so sorry. I did not mean to do that. I love my customers. It's just the work I have to do."

The door opened as Jack said, "I watched how you rang up the last sale. Is there anything else that I need to know?"

She looked at him with a puzzled expression.

"I'm going to stay here for a little while to help you out so that you can get some traction on your other work. If that's okay with you."

Tears started filling her eyes. "I can't pay you, Jack. I'm not at that place in my business."

Tears. He couldn't take it when a woman cried. He rushed to speak. "I'm doing this for a friend."

She nodded at him. While the new customers browsed, she demonstrated the checkout process, both with cash and credit cards. Then she handed him the key to the cases with the more expensive jewelry.

He said in a low voice, "Right now, you take care of your job, and I'll take care of this. Oh, and do you mind if I straighten up the front window? I noticed it seemed a bit chaotic, not like it had been before."

She smiled. "Thank you."

After helping the customers, who turned out to be browsers and not buyers, Jack rearranged the pieces of jewelry in the front window more or less as he remembered her doing it when he'd walked by days ago. Looking around her store, he wondered if there was some additional way he could help her. She seemed to have more work than she could do.

He thought about today and the rest of the week. The fall colors had faded and the leaves had fallen, so the natural landscape wasn't at its finest. There weren't many pictures he needed to shoot until after snow set in. He could find someone to take him out on the water to see if he could get more shots of whales, though. That beauty was not dependent on seasons.

With the case straightened, he closed it back up and locked it. After glancing around, he realized that the wedding ring case wasn't in much better condition than the front. Everything that she'd taken out to store in her safe overnight had been dumped back in. He called out, "Aimee, is it okay with you if I also straighten up the wedding ring case? I more or less remember how you had it when I was here looking at the rings."

Silence greeted him. Maybe he'd crossed the line. She barely knew him, and he was working with her most expensive jewelry pieces. He was about to open his mouth to say he was sorry for being pushy when she replied.

"Thank you, Jack. That would be great."

He went to work and straightened that up. His phone buzzed with a call and he answered.

"Jack, aren't you coming for lunch?" his mother asked over the line.

He checked the time on his watch. Almost noon. "I'm sorry, Mom! I'm helping someone and lost track of time. I'll definitely be there next week."

"I'm going to make you promise."

He grinned. "I promise. Tell everyone hello for me."

"I will. Next week, your father is helping someone build a small weekend getaway cabin on the Kenai River, and he's supposed to be there Saturday. Our family lunch is being moved to Sunday after church."

"I can come then. But you know you could seal the deal with a blueberry pie."

She laughed. "Have you talked to your father lately?" She didn't give him time to reply before going on. "We picked blueberries last weekend, and I froze them. I can use those, or we could go out again this week. I love berry picking!"

"My mouth is watering. I'll be there!" He said goodbye and hung up.

A few minutes later, Aimee stepped into the room, shrugged her shoulders and stretched. "I've been sitting a while and need to move." As she leaned first to the right and then the left, she said, "Jack, can I be honest with you for a minute?"

He nodded.

"Business is almost too good. I can handle either the customers or the work at the jewelry bench. The custom work—the special jobs that I have right now—is taking a lot of time."

Now he understood. "What are you working on?"

She smiled again. "I'm creating a wedding set for the sweetest couple. There are a lot of stones in the rings along with intricate engraving and granulation. I think they will be gorgeous when they're done, but . . ."

Jack knew the definition of everything she'd just said, right down to the process for making the tiny gold beads known as granulation. But he didn't have the skills to do such detailed, specialty work. He was more of a bench basics kind of guy with repairs such as new prongs on a diamond's setting or sizing a ring. He could even go so far as to set a diamond in a brand-new ring, but he didn't have these high-level jewelry skills. Any time he could have spent acquiring them was time he'd used to refine his photography skills. And that had eventually pulled him away from the jewelry business.

"I'll stay a couple of hours. Will that help?"

"So much!" She stepped forward, and he hoped he'd get another hug. She must have caught herself because she stopped with one foot in the air and slowly lowered it to the floor. "I'd better get working." She smiled and went to the back room.

He got back into the groove of being in retail with the surprise that he enjoyed some parts of it. He no longer had the responsibility of the whole business, and he didn't have to be here six days a week. As soon as he could, though, he'd be glad to go back to his new normal life, to discover beauty around the next corner and shoot photos of it. Right now, he could tell that Aimee didn't like needing help, but she did.

When Aimee had handed Jack the keys to the cases, she'd been glad that Bree Kinkaid had vouched for this man. She sat at her workbench, took a deep breath in, and let it out slowly.

She loved being behind the bench and creating jewelry. But every time she was interrupted, she had to find her way back into the project, and there had been a lot of interruptions lately. Good for business, not so good for artistic creativity or for making sure that nothing was forgotten in the fabrication process.

She blinked back tears, but her vision blurred. She went over to her desk and grabbed a tissue, dabbing at her eyes. Bree Kincaid had sent her an angel in the form of Jack O'Connell. If she could just have a couple of uninterrupted hours, she might feel like she was getting somewhere on this wedding ring set.

She hadn't thought about how much time it would take to run everything when she'd opened her store. She'd assumed she'd figure it all out. *Joneses always figure it out. We're fighters.* She'd heard her grandfather and parents say that many times. She felt her dream slipping away, though, in spite of how enthusiastic she'd felt after Molly's pep talk yesterday. Maybe she wouldn't be able to figure it out. She might disappoint herself and her family with her failure.

The door's bell chimed a few times every hour as she

worked, and each time she'd hear voices as Jack greeted them. For free.

When lunchtime came, he called out, "Aimee, did you bring a lunch, or do you usually eat out?"

She pushed back from her bench and went out to the larger room. "I usually bring a lunch, but—"

"You didn't have time this morning."

She shrugged. "Nope. I rolled out of bed and came straight here."

"Well, if you can stay up here for a few minutes, I could go back to Cinnamon Bakery. I noticed that they make sandwiches too."

She didn't want to stop working long enough to get her own lunch, so she either had to ask Molly to step away during a busy time or allow Jack to go. There wasn't another option. "Give me the veggie special on whole-wheat with extra cheese. And another large cup of coffee wouldn't hurt."

Jack hurried up the sidewalk to the coffee shop and wondered what he was doing here. Aimee had needed help, he was sure of that. But why had *he* offered to help? Of course, he'd been the one who brought home Fluffy the kitten when he'd found her wandering in an empty lot on his way home from kindergarten. His family had adopted her, but they never let him forget that he'd been the one to bring in the stray. And he'd gotten in a fight in junior high when one of the big kids was picking on a smaller one, and he'd stepped in to help. Then there was his last girlfriend. When she'd needed rent money, he'd given her enough to pay for a month. She'd found greener pastures right after that, leaving him feeling like he had been used all along. And he probably had.

He must have *sucker* written on his forehead. Aimee was like the kitten he'd found. Or even the bullied kid. He saw a need, and he had to take care of it. His family called it the *Fluffy Syndrome*.

He entered the bakery and placed their order. Molly was filling coffee for someone at a table, but as soon as she had done that, she came over to him. "Twice in one day?"

"We haven't been formally introduced, but I assume you're Aimee's friend, Molly. Is that right?"

She gave him a long look before answering. "I am."

"I'm helping Aimee out, and we both need something to eat."

At that, both of her eyebrows shot up. "Okaaay." She drew the word out slowly. "I've been planning to stop by after the lunch rush. Let her know I'll do that."

"I will. I'm sure she'll be happy about that."

Molly's expression told him that Aimee was also going to have to explain his presence. He didn't know how she would do that, since he wasn't sure how *he* would explain it. So he just gave Molly their orders and waited the short time it took to make the sandwiches.

With Jack on the lunch run and the store having a momentary lull, Aimee took a moment to consider her day. She realized that Jack needed to leave. The poor man had stopped in to check on his mother's gift and ended up spending half the day working for her.

She had to figure this out on her own. For now, she just

needed to thank this man, who Molly would no doubt ask many questions about, and send him on his way. This situation was her problem. No one could help her. Not even her grandfather, who had been there for her in so many situations. A fishing charter owner did not know anything about jewelry or even retail. Neither did a photographer, even one Bree had said had . . . how had her friend phrased it? Some knowledge of metals? He had done a good job for a beginner, though.

When Jack returned, they ate their sandwiches out front, using a glass jewelry case as a table. Only friends and family received an invitation to her personal space in the back. Aimee looked up at the man in front of her, and boy, was he easy on the eyes. He was not only handsome, but he also seemed to be a really nice man. "How are your brothers doing? Did Maddie like her rings?"

"The rings are perfect for each of them. You did a great job figuring out what she would want based on my description."

She chuckled. "When you described her as having eyes the color of Kachemak Bay, I thought you had fallen in love hard."

His eyes widened in surprise, and then he chuckled. "The photographer in me saw her that way."

When they'd finished, she wadded up the sandwich wrappers and said, "Thank you, Jack. Your help made today much better. I'll be able to manage now."

He watched her for a moment. "I was happy to help. You're sure you don't need me to stick around a bit longer?"

She smiled broadly, at least she hoped that's what it looked like. "I'm fine. Thank you again." It made her inexplicably sad when he left. But she went back to work and soon forgot about her helper.

When the door chimed after a short reprieve, Aimee took a deep breath and stepped out the door from the back room into her store, smiling as broadly as she could at the older woman. "May help you?"

Her customer explained what she needed, and Aimee thankfully had something that would be perfect. She didn't know when she'd be able to pay for all of the pre-made jewelry in her store, but she hoped she earned enough to do that soon. Every little sale nibbled away at her debt. But it took time away from her bench too.

The door dinged behind her customer, and she gave her a happy wave when she glanced back as the door closed. The woman smiled and waved back. Aimee knew her reputation was growing in Homer, and she liked that. She wanted to not only serve the visitors but also the people who lived here.

Jack had been beyond kind to help her today. She realized that her temporary break had calmed her down, but instead of fixing the situation, it had given her the benefit of a sound mind and the ability to realize she had a major problem. She wasn't sure how she was going to be able to finish the work she had in front of her in the amount of time she had.

She was in a situation that she hadn't expected to be in. She had plenty of business, but not enough time to take care of it. And not enough business to hire someone to help her so that she could get the work done.

CHAPTER FIVE

*a*imee shifted her big mug of coffee, a.k.a. her morning energy, so that she could reach into her pocket for the hair tie she knew she'd put there, only to find the pocket empty. She must have taken it out and set it down somewhere the night before. It should have been easy when you considered that she was wearing the same pants that she'd worn yesterday and probably the day before.

She unlocked the door to her jewelry store an hour before she'd normally arrive, relocked it, then hurried through the room to turn off the alarm. Once done, she went into the backroom. The calendar hanging near her work-bench had a circle around Saturday, the day that she had to have this wedding set ready, and an x on every day since the bride had called about the elopement.

Today was Monday, and these rings had to be done by Saturday morning at the latest. She'd done what would normally be unthinkable and come to work on Sunday immediately after church. Giving the carpet a glance, she decided it could go another day without being vacuumed, but she did grab her spray cleaner and give the top of the glass cases a good wiping down. Then she headed to the back to get the jewelry out of the safe.

She dumped some of it into the front display, stopping to upright a couple of pieces. There wasn't really a way to shove the tray into the wedding ring case and dump it, but she put the rings into the case as fast as she could. It was better to have it displayed than not, right? At least that's what she told herself as she walked away and did not look back.

She took the box with an ever-growing number of jobs out of the safe and set it on the top of her jewelry bench. The long line of yellow envelopes stared back at her and seemed to mock her. She took the one at the front out—the wedding rings—and went back to work on them.

She'd planned to get this part of the job done on Saturday but had been interrupted too many times. Now, she began the careful task of hand engraving a delicate pattern that added an elegant touch to the rings. An hour later, she got up, unlocked the front door, and flipped the sign to *open*. Then she went back to work.

Much too soon, the bell sounded over the door, and she walked out, wiping her hands on her jeans and giving what she hoped was a cheerful smile. A family bought several pieces of jewelry to take home with them to Des Moines. As soon as she got settled in her chair again after finishing with their sale, the doorbell chimed again. She got up and helped another customer, this time someone local who needed baby earrings. She was glad she had bought some for her inventory.

After ten minutes of work, the door sounded again. She pulled her magnifying visor off and pressed her hands against her forehead. At this rate, she would have a full cash register from jewelry sales, but angry people whose custom work kept being delayed. And how could she not have rings ready for someone's special moment? She stood and trudged out front while gluing on her best smile, which she suspected was none too good at this point. She was probably going to have to pull some all-nighters—staying awake twenty-four hours or more—in order to get this done.

Jack had avoided the jewelry store for a couple of days, but walking past it now, he saw a display case that was even worse than before. It had become his barometer for Aimee's life. She must need help. He pushed open the door and heard sounds coming from a back room. "Hello?" he called. There was a pause in the noise and then a different sound, probably a chair scooting backward.

Aimee came out of a doorway, running her fingers through her normally tamed but now messy hair. She looked exhausted. What had happened to her? She said, "Can I help you with anything?" before she was near enough to recognize him.

As she walked closer to him, he could see how tired she looked. The jewelry store must be struggling, but he'd seen many people in Homer today who appeared to be visitors, so she should be earning a good income. How should he approach this?

"Jack? How are you?"

She looked down to the floor and then up at him, blinking furiously as though she was trying to hold back tears.

"Are you okay, Aimee? Is something wrong with a friend or family member?"

She shook her head. "No. Everyone is healthy. When I left my grandparents this morning, my grandfather was out chopping firewood to build up his stockpile for the winter." Talking about him, she smiled for the first time since he'd arrived, and her eyes lit up. When she glanced around the room, the look of sadness came into her eyes again.

"I saw the window display . . ."

"It's a mess, right? I don't have time to fix it. A group of six from Iowa just left, and it was busy all morning leading up to them." She blinked again, and he battled between pulling her into a comforting hug and the instinctive male urge to run far and fast away from a weepy woman. But Aimee clearly needed help.

"Aimee, I'm a guy, and guys don't really want to get into these emotional situations, but it seems like there's a problem with the store, and I might be able to help with that."

She stood, wringing her hands for a moment before speaking. "You already helped me. But I might need more expertise now than you can offer." She took a step backward. "Not that I don't appreciate the offer."

"Until February, I owned a jewelry store in Fairbanks. I've been in the business for years."

"Oh." She studied him for a moment. "Why didn't you mention that before?"

Why hadn't he? "I don't know. I guess it didn't matter."

She pursed her lips for a moment, then said, "If I could talk to someone who understands what I do, that might be good."

"Why don't I get coffee and something sweet from the bakery? You can take a break and talk to me."

She glanced over her shoulder toward, he assumed, the area with her workbench. With a big sigh, she turned back toward him and said, "I don't think I *should* take a break."

"Aimee, you need to stop for a few minutes. Everyone needs to do that occasionally."

"No! No! I have got to get this done on time!" She shook her head vigorously from side to side as she spoke.

He put one hand on each of her shoulders. "Look at me, Aimee."

She looked up at him.

"I'm going to go get some coffee for us. Would you like a cinnamon roll?"

She rubbed her hand over her face. "I don't know, Jack. I can't think straight." She looked back up at him, and her sad eyes tore through his defenses. What was going on with this woman? "Just tell Molly to give me my favorite coffee and a sweet treat." She looked around. "I'm not sure where I set my purse this morning, but let me get you some money—"

"I've got this. Just sit and relax, and I'll be back in a few minutes."

She gave a slow nod, then turned and slowly went back to the doorway through which she'd entered a few minutes ago. It was a good thing he had stopped in this morning because she was about ready for a meltdown.

He went out the door and down the street to the bakery. Inside, he found Molly straightening her display case.

"Hi, Molly."

Aimee's friend turned toward him when he spoke.

"Aimee's been working too hard. I stopped in, and she

looked so stressed out that I said I'd come here to get the coffee she likes and a sweet treat."

Molly's hand covered her mouth. "Is she okay?"

"Yes, but you might want to stop in later."

She bustled around the area, making coffee for her friend, then paused. "How do you like yours?"

"I've been getting black coffee, but I'd like something else today. Do you do fancy coffees?"

She raised one eyebrow. "I wouldn't have picked you for a fancy coffee guy, but, yes, I do."

He grinned. "Then make me whatever is your favorite right now. And I would like a cinnamon roll with that."

She soon handed him a box and then a carrier with the two coffees in it. When he took out his wallet, she said, "No. This one's on me. I'm glad you're helping her. I don't know anything about jewelry. And tell Aimee that I'll definitely be by later today to check on her."

He gave her a nod and went out the door.

Back at Homer Gems, he found Aimee waiting on a customer. She must have checked the mirror after he'd left because her hair was combed and her shirt straightened. He set their snacks down on a glass case and waited for her. Her smile seemed strained today. When the customer left, she slowly walked over to him again, moving as though it took great effort.

He glanced around, and the only chairs he saw were the two in front of the diamond case. "Do you have anywhere for two people to sit in the back?"

She seemed to be weighing her options.

"I'm not a customer anymore," he said gently. "I used to own a jewelry store, so there's nothing scary about a back room or a jewelry bench."

Her eyes did light up at that moment. "I'd forgotten." She started for the back room and waved him on. "It's a mess back here. You may want to wipe off the chair to make sure there isn't polishing compound on it."

He chuckled when he stepped into the back room. Contrary to what she thought, it was one of the neatest office-and-bench areas he'd ever seen. She had a small desk and chair to the right when you walked through the doorway. Two jeweler's benches with chairs were to his left, one workbench clearly in use and the other empty. "This is a great space back here. And you have *two* benches?"

She frowned as she stared at the second one that was currently completely clean and unoccupied. "When I opened this store, I thought that if I was going to have one desk shipped, I may as well make it two. My plan is to have someone else work with me and take over the day-to-day repairs and simple jewelry making."

He shuddered. "Ring sizing."

She grinned. "Not my favorite job, either. There's nothing really bad about it, though. It's just repetitive, and every repetitive job gets tedious after a while." She spun her bench chair around, and he sat down on the other one, pulling it far away from the actual bench.

The setting was bringing back memories, and they weren't the happiest ones of his life. He'd wanted to escape that store for so long so he could do what he truly loved. No day in his life had made him happier than when he'd signed the papers to sell his store, been handed his check—with, to his surprise, a profit—and walked away from there. He'd also hated being so far away from his family. Sure, it was still in the same state, but he could have driven from Chicago to Nashville in the same amount of time, crossing multiple states in the Lower Forty-Eight. Here, it was the distance between two towns in a very large state.

She popped open the lid on the coffee, took a sip, and closed her eyes with a sigh. When she opened them, she looked over at Jack. "Thank you. I hadn't realized that I needed an intervention. And I barely know you."

"One of my brothers came for a surprise visit a couple of years ago. He found me overworked and not getting out, but he remedied that before he left town. Sometimes we need others to help us."

She nodded, then took another sip of her coffee and looked into the bag of treats. "Whew. Molly gave me one of her caramel apple cupcakes. She only created this one a couple of weeks ago, and I oohed and aahed over the test batch."

He took a bite of his cinnamon roll. "She's a genius with baked goods."

Each drank their coffee and ate their sweets in silence, but it was a pleasant silence. He was glad she wasn't someone who felt the need to fill every quiet moment. When she'd finished, she stood up. "I'm going to wash my hands, and then I can get back to work. I am feeling better, Jack. Thank you."

Jack looked around when she was gone. Her love of pretty had made its way back here. It wasn't as over-the-top as what his mother did, though. The walls were a soft blue. About the only décor was a cute calendar topped with a photo of kittens with the upcoming Saturday circled. This was more livable, even for a guy. When she was done, he went into the bathroom and washed his hands. Molly had provided a fork, but he'd still managed to get sticky.

When he stepped out, he started to leave and then looked

back over at Aimee. She focused on the work in front of her. The doorbell chimed, she dropped the metal on the bench and got up to take care of her customer. He followed her out of the back so he would not be left alone there with her jobs. That would have bothered him when he had his store. He was still a stranger to her. He watched from the side of the room as she sold the couple a simple necklace for their daughter's birthday, gift wrapped it, and handed it them it to them with a smile. That shallow smile again.

When she went to the back, he followed her there. "I can tell you're overwhelmed. I wish I could help."

She watched him for a moment with a steady eye. "That's enough about me for right now. How is your photography business going?"

The abrupt shift caught him off guard, but he'd go with it. Maybe she needed to talk about something else for a minute. "I've been just about anywhere with a road in Alaska this summer. But I'm very happy to be back in Homer."

"There's no place like Homer, is there?"

He chuckled at the saying that the visitor center had come up with at some point. "No, there's no place like Homer. And I don't even have to click my heels to get here."

"Where are you off to next?"

"I'm here for a while. When I sold the store in Fairbanks, I also sold my house there. I've found a temporary place to live, but I'm hoping to find a place to call my own soon."

Aimee hesitated for a moment before asking, "So . . . nothing big is happening today?"

Jack studied her for a moment. This question seemed to be important to her. What was he missing? "I'm going to take photos this week—as many as my heart desires. I've been able to sell most of what I consider my best work."

She wrung her hands and looked down at the floor again before looking up at him and asking in a tiny voice, "Would you be able to help me today?" She waved her hands in front of herself. "Just so I can get a little caught up. I know it's a lot to ask, but . . ."

When he did not reply immediately, she stood straighter and put her shoulders back. "Pretend that I never asked that. You sold your business. It's my job to make my business work."

Jack cringed at the thought of being chained to the hours of a retail business again. That had been his biggest mistake in life. Just because you love something doesn't mean that you want to do it six or seven days a week, every week, with no end in sight. But she was blinking furiously again, and he felt like she was going to start crying the second she was alone. Something in him spoke up. "I can help. But I'm not as good on the bench as you are."

Aimee smiled, and when this woman really smiled, her face lit up. "Are you sure?" She seemed to sense his hesitation because she asked again, "Please tell me if you really mean this, Jack. I only need help out front right now. I thought about asking a friend or family member to help, but no one I know other than you has a background in jewelry. They wouldn't be able to answer any questions or make suggestions beyond the basics for the customers. I think I'd lose a lot of money on that. But you—"

"I know a lot about jewelry, Aimee. I can easily help with your customers. How far behind are you on your jobs?"

She picked up a narrow box on her workbench that had yellow job envelopes lined up in it. There had to be a dozen or more of them.

His eyes widened as he stared at it. "Are these all custom work?"

Staring at the box, she sat down hard in her chair and set the box where it belonged. "Jack, I have gotten so far behind over the summer. My customers have been patient with me, but for how long? This wedding set can't wait. The couple came in, and I designed rings for them. They said they were getting married in December. Then the bride contacted me last week and told me they had decided to elope in a week and a half. I have until Saturday, so I've been here from sunup to sundown almost every day. I've barely had time to eat, and you don't want to know the last time I took a shower."

He laughed. "If it helps, you look just as good to me as you always do." He realized that might have sounded wrong and even inappropriate. "What I meant to say was—"

She grinned. "It's okay. Either I always look bad. Or I managed to look okay in spite of the fact that I'm not bathing on a regular basis."

At least she hadn't read anything romantic into his words. Romance wasn't even on his radar right now. He'd help her today and walk away.

CHAPTER SIX

*A*imee held her phone in front of her and stared at it. The screen showed a call, so she wasn't hallucinating due to exhaustion. "Excuse me? Could you please repeat what you just said?"

The groom half of the custom wedding ring couple said, "I wanted to make sure that Sherry gave you the correct date. Our flight to Vegas from Anchorage leaves very early on Saturday, so we'll need to pick up the rings on Friday."

That's what she thought she'd heard. "I've been working toward Saturday as the pickup date." As soon as she said the words, she regretted them.

"Oh, no! We can't get married without rings. Should we buy other rings? Something that's already made? Maybe we should do that when we get to Anchorage."

Forcing a calm note into her voice, calm she was a long way from feeling, she said, "I'll have them ready for you. Don't worry."

"Are you sure?" She heard muffled sounds like he'd

covered the phone with his hand, and his next words could barely be heard. "Sherry, she might not finish the rings on time."

A shriek came through loud and clear.

Aimee jumped to her feet. "Don't worry! Your beautiful, custom rings will be ready for you on Friday."

"You're sure?" A bit of distrust had crept into his voice.

"Absolutely!" She punched her fist into the air, giving every ounce of energy she had for that one word. "You will *love* your rings." When he remained quiet, she added, "I *promise* they'll be done on time."

That must be what he'd needed. "I accept your promise. Can we pick them up at noon on Friday?"

She thought about it for a second. "Yes. I'll have them ready. I'm excited for you to see them."

"We are too." Now, she could hear his happiness. "Sherry, she promised they'll be done."

This time, his fiancée made a happy squeal.

They hung up, and Aimee dropped the phone on her chair. She'd just promised something close to impossible. And she might ruin her business if she didn't follow through with that promise. An online review of a wedding ring designer who didn't finish the rings on time would be a red flag to potential customers.

She checked her watch. Eleven o'clock. She had most of today, tomorrow, and Friday morning to finish these rings.

Jack tucked his cameras into the trunk and closed it. He'd managed to steer clear of Homer Gems yesterday so that he would avoid his rescuer tendencies. Aimee had said she was okay at the end of the day on Monday, and he hoped she'd been honest.

His curiosity got the best of him—at least he decided to call it curiosity. When an amazing cup of coffee from Cinnamon Bakery came to mind, he parked his vehicle up the street so he would have to walk by Homer Gems. At the jewelry store, he stopped cold. The front case was empty. Its sliding door, which should have been closed and locked, stood open.

Cupping his hands on the glass so that he could see inside, he found the store empty inside. Maybe she'd decided to close the store for a day to recover from her hard work. She would lose some business, but it might have been her best option. He went over to the door and found no sign saying she'd closed, so he pulled on it, and it opened.

Aimee didn't appear. He went to the back and found her hunched over her workbench, working on a ring.

"Aimee?"

She dropped the tool that she'd been using and jumped. Looking up at him and blinking, she seemed to be trying to focus on him. "I'm sorry. The bell must be broken because I didn't hear you come in."

She had dark circles under her eyes. A couple of crumpled up bags littered the floor beside her and had probably held snacks or meals at some point.

"Aimee, the bell works. Are you okay?"

She gave a slow nod, and then halfway through, turned her head from side to side instead. "Jack, I'm not. Do you remember my customers who decided to elope?"

He shrugged. "Sure. Are they having a normal wedding instead?"

"No! They called me early yesterday and moved it up a day. Their flight leaves from Anchorage Saturday morning, so they need to pick up the rings Friday. *Friday!* I lost a whole day. There are no shortcuts with these. Every step takes time." She rubbed her eyes with the back of her hand. "I was starting to feel like I had everything under control when that happened. But why are you here?"

He sighed. The whole situation was Fluffy all over again. No. This was worse than Fluffy because he had been able to take care of the kitten and change her life forever. He could not do that with Aimee, no matter how much Bree Kincaid, the would-be matchmaker, wanted that. Besides, he doubted that Aimee would want to be taken care of so much as she'd want to find someone to love her and share a life as equals, just as he would.

"Aimee, there isn't any jewelry in the front case."

She squinted and looked up at him as though she was trying to sort out what he had just said. "I remember opening the safe and taking everything out so that I could put it in the cases." She pushed her chair away from her desk and stood. "I also remember putting rings in one of the cases." She went out to the front of the store, and he followed her.

She gasped and pointed. A tray of jewelry sat on the front glass case. "Anyone could have walked in, picked it up, and walked out with the most expensive part of my inventory." She blinked her eyes furiously and turned away from him as he heard a small sob. "I can't believe I did that. You must think I'm an idiot."

"No, I think you're exhausted, and you're trying to do more than is humanly possible."

When she sniffled again and then sobbed, he didn't know what to do. He wanted to hug her, but that was far from

63

appropriate. "Maybe you should close for today or for the rest of the week so that you can get caught up."

She wheeled around. Tears streamed down her face. "I can't do that, Jack. I am earning money from my custom work, but I have to pay the rent, the overhead like utilities, and for the merchandise you see."

Some people stopped outside the jewelry store, then turned, looked inside, and pointed at the empty front case. They shrugged and came over to the door. Aimee brushed at her cheeks and tried to force a smile.

"I'll handle this. You go to the back and pull yourself together."

Aimee whispered, "Thank you, Jack." She rushed to the back.

Jack moved the jewelry to the side, away from any customers' reach, and greeted the people as they came in the door. He helped them with their purchase and stood behind the counter, watching them leave and wondering what he should do. What *could* he do? He didn't own this jewelry store.

Should he make decisions for her? He glanced toward the back and realized that she needed a friend. He could get Molly from the bakery, but Molly had admitted that she didn't know diddly about jewelry. Sighing, he picked up the tray of jewelry for the front window, placed it somewhat artfully in the display, then went to the back. He assumed she'd leave the safe open during the day, but she'd locked it. "Aimee, the wedding jewelry isn't out front, and I can't get into the safe."

She put down the tool and gave him her attention. "The safe is always open when I'm here." She went over to it and stared at it for a few seconds before trying the handle. "It is locked." She spun the dial, opened it, and stepped back. "I'm going to trust you. Thank you for helping."

He grabbed the tray of jewelry, put it away, and picked up the glass cleaner.

She was not going to like charity, and that's what his helping out would seem to be. With the jewelry store put back in order and the cases cleaned, he went to the back to tell her what he had done.

When he stepped through the doorway, he found her, as expected, hunched over her jewelry bench and focused on her work. She might be tired, but her movements were exact and careful. He'd have to ask her about her training some-time when she was less stressed out. He was a competent jeweler, but she was more in the class of a master jeweler.

He cleared his throat to get her attention. She didn't look up. "Aimee?" He said in a low voice so that he wouldn't startle her this time. No movement. She was focused on her work and so exhausted she wasn't seeing or hearing anything beyond it.

He went out to the front and opened and closed the door to make the bell chime. Then he came to the back and stood in the doorway. She hadn't flinched. She was still working on the piece of jewelry. She needed to have the store open, but until she got this set of rings done, she wouldn't be able to run the store. A solution came to mind, not one he loved, but in true Fluffy style, it was the right thing to do.

"Aimee?" He said much louder than he had before.

She dropped her tool again. "You didn't have to shout."

"I actually did. You didn't hear me before, and you also did not hear the bell when I tried that."

Heart-wrenching sorrow crossed her face. "I thought I could do this, Jack. I really did. But I don't think I'm going to make it in business. And I can't allow you to work anymore for free." She pulled off her magnifying jewelry visor and closed her eyes.

He debated his plan and realized he had no option. Someone else might decide that they didn't have to do it, but that was not Jack O'Connell. "Aimee, I have an idea." He sighed. Then he told himself, *Just do it, O'Connell!* "Would you be willing to trade my working here for part of the labor in making Mom's necklace?"

There. He'd said it. Now, he'd be caught up in her business for another day. Why couldn't he have stayed quiet?

She looked toward him, and a flicker of hope glimmered in her eyes. "I'll give you all of the labor for the necklace if you can help me today."

"I can't let you do that. But you'd be paying me if you gave me part of it."

She jumped to her feet and raced over to him. "Thank you!" She pulled him into a hug and squeezed him tightly. Then she stepped back and stared up at him. "You saved my life, Jack. I can't thank you enough."

He stared into her eyes, her pretty blue eyes. Everything about her was pretty and feminine, except for the chipped fingernails with black polishing compound under them that reminded him of her profession. But somehow, she even managed to carry that off with style. He reached over and brushed a few stray strands of hair off her forehead. When his eyes looked down to her mouth, and she started to lean forward, the bell chimed over the door, and he jumped back.

He rushed to leave, saying, "I'll get that. I'm your

employee now. Just let me know if you need me to do anything else."

~

Aimee watched Jack as he hurried out to help her customers. She'd almost kissed Jack O'Connell. Or rather he'd almost kissed her. Or had he? Her muddled brain couldn't even sort through the basics. She should certainly be able to tell if a handsome man had almost kissed her, shouldn't she?

She turned and went back toward her chair. Sitting down, she picked up the piece of jewelry and put on her jewelry visor. Without having to consider it for long, she knew exactly what to do next on the ring. If she hadn't trained at the side of a master jeweler for years, to the point that her brain knew what to do even when she was exhausted, she'd be in trouble right now.

She had already fused the gold beads to the ring, then set tiny diamonds in every other bead. Other than final polishing, setting the large round diamond in the center would be the final step for that ring. All three rings were coming to life. Normally, she might have been able to ask her customers to give her a grace period and delay the wedding band for a while because it wouldn't be needed until the day of the ceremony, but an elopement did not allow for that. These had to be finished by Friday at noon, or she was going to ruin a wedding.

She heard footsteps every once in a while and noticed motion out of her peripheral vision, but Jack never talked to her or interrupted, until he said, "Aimee?"

She looked up from her bench. How much time had passed?

"I put everything away."

She shook her head and shrugged. "Put everything away?"

"Your open hours on the door say you close at six, so I took everything out of the cases, and that jewelry is now in the safe. Is there anything else that I need to do before we leave?"

Before *we* leave? Hysterical laugher started to bubble up inside her. Leave? She turned toward Jack and said, "I think I'm going to be here a little while still. Why don't you go home?"

"You're exhausted. I suspect that you're going to start making mistakes, even if you normally would not. I think it's time to go home."

"Jack, I've never been the damsel in distress type. I can handle this. Go home."

He straightened his shoulders and watched her for a moment before answering. "How much longer do you think you can work before you're too exhausted to sit there?"

She struggled to find the answer in her head. If she worked even another forty-five minutes, she'd be able to set the center diamond. Then she could work on the groom's ring in the morning. "Maybe forty-five minutes. An hour tops."

He stared at her as though he was trying to sort something out in his head. "I'll stay and help you close up."

Her new help was pushing her buttons. "I can take care of myself, Jack. I'll say it again, go home!"

"Why don't I work on some of the small jobs you have while you work on that? That will help you get ahead, and we won't be distracted by anyone coming into the store now that we're closed."

She was about to protest the use of the word *we,* but she

knew he was right and that any help would be a blessing beyond compare. "You have a deal. I apparently had visions of grandeur when I set this up, so not only is the workbench ready, the torch is there, everything you need should be there. You might have to share my tools, though."

"Do you have any ring sizings that need to be done or anything of that nature?"

She pointed to her job box. "Sort through the jobs. They're in order from oldest in front to newest in the back, and I've written clear directions for the work needed on each."

Jack put on the apron she had lying over the spare chair and then sat down, picked up the box, and chose an envelope. She waited for him to ask her a million questions. When he just got to work like he knew what he was doing, her shoulders relaxed, and she went back to her own job. She finished what she felt like she needed to get done that night, dropped the ring into its envelope, and pushed back from her workbench.

He lifted his visor and looked over at her. "Are we done?"

She struggled again with the *we* word but answered. "I finished the engagement ring. I'm almost done with the wedding band, but the groom's ring still has some work to do."

Jack removed his visor. "I finished two jobs and just need to do a bit of a polish on this third one. I'll do that in the morning, then I can call them to let them know that their work is ready."

She chewed her lip and thought about it. "I think I should call them. I want them to see me as the voice and face of Homer Gems."

"That's sensible." He stood and took off his apron, laying

69

it down on the chair where she'd kept it because she hoped to have help someday. "Where are you parked? It's getting late, so I'll walk you to your car."

Instead of feeling her hackles rising again because he was trying to help, she appreciated that. It's something her grandfather would have done. She took a step and stumbled a bit, reaching out to hold on to the side of her bench for stability. Her grip tightened when she felt her knees start to give out.

Jack hurried to her side. "Tell me what's going on, Aimee."

She shook her head to clear it. "I'm tired—no, scratch that —I'm exhausted. I know I just had coffee for breakfast, and there's a strong possibility that I forgot about lunch."

He pointed at the wadded up bag on the floor.

"I'm sure that was from yesterday's lunch. Molly stopped by with something."

What was she going to do? She'd gotten herself into this. Now, how was she going to get herself out of it? So much for being a responsible businesswoman. She'd been dreaming of this business for years, and now she'd gotten herself into a mess when she was just getting started.

A tiny voice reminded her that she'd been dreaming of *making jewelry* for years, not necessarily of a retail storefront.

She put her shoulders back and stood straight. If anyone could manage this situation by sheer will, it was her. She had hiked twenty miles in a day and spent ten or twelve hours on a fishing boat multiple times. She took a step and then another and another, walking straight for the door and her escape.

~

70

Jack watched Aimee heading for the door. The woman had drive and guts; he'd say that about her for sure. He wasn't sure that she was going to be able to get herself home, though. "Aimee, we need to set the alarm and lock the safe. I think that's it unless I'm missing something."

She stopped where she was and reached out for the nearby counter to support herself. "Please put the box with the jobs from my desk into the safe, too, along with the tray of gemstones. Then just flip the handle up and spin the dial. The alarm is set from out here. I'm probably a completely crazy woman for trusting you after knowing you such a short time, but I'm going to trust Bree and the fact that she is related to you."

He took care of the safe. When he went into the retail area from the back, she pointed to her right toward the alarm panel. She said the code out loud, he entered it, and then she started for the door again on wobbly feet. He pulled the door open and helped her out. After watching her try three times to get her key in the lock, he took the keyring from her and locked the door.

"Okay, where's your car?"

He knew she did not want help from anyone and could see the battle she was waging in her mind. Then she pointed to the right. "I parked a few blocks that direction."

"I'm one block in the other direction. I came for a cup of coffee and thought I should check to see what was going on with you. And here we are."

She looked up at him and squinted.

"Aimee, how many hours did you work yesterday?"

She looked down and then back up at him. "I've been working since yesterday." Her voice was so quiet he could barely hear it.

Had she said what he thought she had? "Aimee, are you saying that you worked for thirty-six hours straight?"

"Jack, if those rings aren't finished, I'm going to ruin a wedding. And I will probably ruin my business and everything that I've worked toward for years. I can't let that happen over a little sleep."

"I can see what you're saying, but you're so exhausted that I don't know what to do right now. The one thing I do know is that I'm going to have to drive you home. I don't think you can drive yourself."

A quiet voice said, "You may be right, Jack. I could call my grandfather and have him come get me. We live pretty far up East End road."

Jack lived near the start of the East End road and knew it led to some of the most beautiful views around Homer. The road cut just above the coastline with houses on each side of it and a hill rising up to the left. He'd tried to find a rental further out there, but they'd either been ridiculously expensive or not something he wanted to call home. Maybe he'd be able to move there in a couple of years when he'd built his photography business up even more.

He looked at the woman in front of him. She made beautiful jewelry and was probably great at business under normal circumstances, but she'd been pushed pretty far on this. Custom rings were not usually done in a hurry for an elopement.

"I'll drive you. Let's go this way."

Aimee stumbled along beside him, and he finally put his arm around her to help support her as she walked. She seemed to almost fall asleep at one point, so he picked her up in his arms and carried her.

"Jack, I can walk."

"Aimee, it's taking us a really long time to walk one block. That's my SUV up ahead." She turned her head to the left. "I'm driving the black SUV." He had never carried a woman before but was enjoying the feel of having Aimee in his arms close to his chest. *Don't go there, O'Connell!*

He set her on her feet, supporting her with one arm so that he could open the door. She started to slide down, so he scooped her up again and plopped her onto the front seat.

When he got into the vehicle, she was leaning back with her eyes closed, so he wasn't even sure she was awake anymore. It didn't matter for a little while because he did know how to get to the East End road. On the way, he drove past the grocery store he'd planned to stop at to get dinner supplies, so his meal later would be skimpy.

When she snorted softly, he knew she'd fallen asleep. About ten minutes later, he nudged her shoulder. "Aimee." He said the word softly and hoped it would get through her sleepiness. With no other distractions, it did, because she opened her eyes, blinked, and looked around. When she saw him, she jumped to the side of the seat and stared at him.

"It's okay. It's just me, Jack, taking you home. Do you remember that?"

She seemed to be searching her brain for information and then had a look of recognition. "Yes, I'm sorry. When I woke up in a strange place, I didn't know what was going on."

"Understandable, but you're safe here. I don't even have a criminal record."

She grinned at that.

"But I do need directions. We're on the East End road, and I've been driving on it for a while. Where's your grandfather's house?"

She looked around, and a minute later, she said, "We still

73

have a mile or so to go. It'll be on the left. You're looking for a white house on a hill, and it's fairly large. It's an older house, so it has more of a farmhouse style, but there are big windows in the front, and the mailbox has pansies planted around it."

He continued driving until he found that spot and pulled up the gravel drive.

CHAPTER SEVEN

A large white house with windows facing the bay greeted him as he drove up the driveway. There was no question about it: Aimee had a beautiful place to live. He glanced over at her to ask more about the house, but she was sound asleep again. He pulled to a stop at the top of the driveway, and she still didn't budge, so he went around to the passenger side and opened it up. "Aimee? You're home."

Nothing.

When he touched her shoulder, she leaned into his hand. He finally reached under her legs and behind her back to lift her up. As he walked up to the front door, painted what appeared to be yellow in the dimming light, it opened, and an older man and woman stood there.

The woman stepped closer. "Has she been in an accident?"

"She worked thirty-six hours straight and was so tired that I had to bring her home." When Aimee rested her head on his shoulder, his heart skipped a beat. He shifted her in his arms, so she'd be more upright. Instead, she sighed and snuggled closer. "Could I lay her down somewhere?"

The woman said, "I'm so sorry. This way." She pushed the door open wider.

Jack followed her through to a living room and put Aimee on the couch. He took a throw draped over the back of a couch and covered her. She snuggled into it and made more of the snort sounds.

Jack bit his lip to block the laughter bubbling up.

Her grandmother chuckled. "Aimee's made that noise when she's sleeping since she was a child. A cousin once recorded her at a sleepover and played it during a big family dinner." The woman turned to look at him with a questioning expression at the same time that the man walked over.

"I'm Jack O'Connell. I've been helping Aimee with her store."

The man's expression so closely resembled Aimee's that Jack knew they had to be related. This was confirmed when the man said, "I'm Carson Jones, and this is my wife, Terri. We're her grandparents. Aimee hasn't mentioned you."

Jack turned to look at his sleeping friend. *Wait, when had he begun thinking of her as a friend?* He'd used that word with her days ago to comfort her, but it seemed that she'd truly become a friend. "I started out as a customer, but I used to own a jewelry store, and she clearly was overwhelmed, so I offered to help this week. I didn't find out how many hours she'd worked until we were leaving, and she couldn't get herself to her own car."

When Aimee fussed a little in her sleep, her grandmother said, "Let's go in the other room. We'll let her sleep off this craziness of hers."

Jack followed them out to the entryway and started to reach for the doorknob when the grandfather—he always had trouble thinking of people his grandparents' age by their first name—said, "Jack, was it?" At Jack's nod, he continued, "I brought home some fresh halibut. Could I talk you into staying for dinner to thank you for bringing our Aimee girl home?"

The delicious smell worked its magic on him, reminding him that he didn't have much to eat at his house and that he wasn't a good cook anyway. Without going back to the store in town, a dinner of oatmeal and a banana that had seen better times were the only things waiting for him. He glanced back at Aimee. He did not think she would appreciate her temporary employee sitting around the dinner table and having a great old time with her grandparents. But then a hint of garlic caught his attention. "I'd be honored. Thank you."

The woman smiled broadly, just like Aimee. She took after both of her grandparents. The two older people started in that direction and waved him on. "We were expecting it to just be family, so I set the table in the kitchen. Very casual."

That appealed to him much more than a formal dinner in a dining room anyway.

A few minutes later, Aimee stumbled into the kitchen, rubbing her sleepy eyes. She stopped in her tracks when she saw Jack. "Why are you here?" she said in an accusatory tone.

Her grandfather said, "Aimee girl, he helped you."

She rubbed her eyes again as if she were trying to clear her vision to see if it really was Jack. "Helped?"

Her grandmother got up and set another place at the table, but instead of putting it on the fourth side as you normally would, she set a place next to Jack. It seemed like there were matchmakers everywhere he went.

"What do you remember about your ride home?" Jack said as he scooted his chair over a few inches to make room for her.

Aimee put her hands on the back of her chair and looked down at the table. "Nothing. I actually remember nothing after I stepped out the door of my store." She looked at her grandparents, put her hand over her mouth, and gasped. "Oh, no! Did I leave my store unlocked?"

"Don't worry. I locked the door, and then I brought you home.

"What about the alarm?"

"You gave me the code, and I set it. Everything's okay."

She stared at him. "I *gave you* the alarm code?"

He shrugged. "You were exhausted, and I was more mobile than you were. Don't worry. Few people remember numbers told them only one time." He smiled in a way he hoped looked sincere.

Looking befuddled, Aimee pulled out her chair and sat down. She picked up her napkin and carefully spread it on her lap. "Well, you're here, and I'm sure I didn't randomly give you the address to my grandparents' home, so that means you must be telling me the truth. Thank you."

"You're welcome. As to why I'm at the table, your grandmother invited me to dinner, and it smelled too fabulous for me to pass it up."

Her grandfather chuckled. "You haven't been misguided by the scent either, my boy. Terri is an amazing cook."

After a short prayer, Aimee's grandmother got up and brought back a plate with halibut fillets on it, set that on the table, then returned with a bowl of potatoes with parsley and butter and another with green beans.

"I want to thank you for your help, Jack," Aimee said as she moved the food around on her plate, but didn't eat. "It was invaluable, and I don't know what I would have done without it."

He ate quietly while he noticed out of the corners of his eyes that each grandparent gave him a questioning expression and glanced from him to their granddaughter. They were getting the wrong idea about his relationship with Aimee. As soon as dinner was over, he pushed back his chair and stood. These were nice people, but he'd done his good deed by bringing Aimee home, and they'd thanked him with the meal. He didn't need any more matchmaking.

Her grandfather rose to his feet. "Don't hurry off, Jack. Come into the living room and visit with us for a while. Our Aimee mentioned something about a jewelry store. Are you her competition?"

Jack laughed. "No, sir. I sold my store in Fairbanks earlier this year. I'm now a nature and wildlife photographer."

Her grandfather put his arm around Jack's shoulders and steered him toward the living room. Jack didn't want to be rude, so he continued in that direction.

When they were seated, Aimee's grandmother said, "Are you visiting Homer?"

"No, ma'am. I've decided to move here. It's always been one of my favorite places. And it's so much warmer in the winter than Fairbanks."

The older woman gave a shudder. "I can't imagine dealing with twenty or thirty or more below zero on a regular basis. We've lived here for about fifty years, though, so we're probably set in our ways. I wouldn't want to live *anywhere* else."

Aimee sat on a chair across from him and watched him with a confused expression on her face. He didn't know if the confusion stemmed from the fact that he was there or that she was completely exhausted and doing her best to focus on the conversation.

"Are you living downtown near the restaurants and where there are lots of things to do? I know that's what young people like."

He grinned. Being lumped in a giant group of "young people" always made him smile because he often didn't think the same way as many others his age. "I'm in a temporary rental right now, but it has an amazing view."

When Aimee leaned forward and almost fell off her chair, he rushed over to grab her at the same time as her grandmother noticed and hurried to the other side.

Aimee's grandmother held onto her granddaughter's shoulder. "I better get my girl to bed. Thank you, Jack O'Connell, for rescuing her. You're welcome to stop by for dinner any time."

He should just leave, but he couldn't without asking one more question. "Do you need help getting her to her room?"

Her grandfather said, "I lift heavy things all the time at work."

"Take his help, Carson."

"I could carry her—" he gave his wife a sweet glare "—but I thank you, Jack. We will accept your offer."

Jack lifted Aimee and followed her grandmother up the stairs and through a doorway. As he moved to set her on the bed, her grandmother said, "Let me take off her shoes first." She did that, and he gently set Aimee down. She sighed as the older woman covered her with the yellow and blue floral bedspread. Aimee seemed so calm now. He hoped tomorrow would be a better day for her.

Downstairs, Jack shook her grandfather's hand.

"It has been a pleasure, son. Don't forget that dinner invitation."

"I may take you up on that sometime. Cooking is not my best skill." With that, he left. The sun was low over the bay and spectacular. He grabbed his cameras out of the trunk and stood in the middle of the front lawn taking pictures until it sank into the water.

CHAPTER EIGHT

*J*ack drove home feeling a little bit like he'd stepped into the story of *Alice in Wonderland*. He had escaped back into reality, but it seemed like Aimee led a pretty charmed life in that house. Now that his duties for Aimee were coming to a close, he used the drive time to consider where he'd like to take photos tomorrow. Inspired by his drive here tonight, he'd go further out the East End Road and stop wherever natural beauty caught his attention.

When he got home, he zipped his jacket against the cool night air as he walked toward the cottage and put his hands in his jacket pockets. His hands hit metal—keys. He took his right hand out and checked to make sure his keys were, as usual, in his pants' pocket. They were. As he wrapped his hand around the other keys, he could feel the shape of a diamond on the key ring.

Pulling the key ring out as he stepped up to his door, he held them up to the porch light, which confirmed what he already knew. They were Aimee's business keys. She might panic when she discovered she didn't have them the next morning because he doubted she'd remember handing them to him. Under normal circumstances, he would call or text her right now, but he didn't think she'd hear a gong going off beside her bed, let alone the small ping of her phone.

His plans for the next day went into the trash can. Oh, well. He'd be a whole lot more upset if this was July when he needed to take pictures of fireweed in bloom or bears frolicking in a field, photos he'd found sold quickly, and that brought in steady income.

When it came to Homer, though, he would never tire of standing on the shore waiting for the sunrise and snapping photo after photo, hoping for the exact right image to appear in his camera. If tomorrow's forecast held, the dawn might be beautiful. Aimee's store didn't open until 9:00 a.m. He could be ready for the sun to rise about 6:30 a.m., stay for an hour, and arrive at Aimee's home long before she needed to open the doors of her business. He didn't know when she'd come out of her sleepy trance, but she should be up by then.

He went inside, got a bottle of water, and sat down on the one comfortable chair. After pulling out a pad of paper, he began listing the places he wanted to take photos of in the next few weeks. Thoughts of his time at Aimee's jewelry store kept creeping in. It hadn't been as terrible as he had imagined. He'd managed to sneak in some photos, not many but a few.

Besides, he didn't seem to be able to fight his Fluffy Syndrome instincts. He'd rarely seen anyone as needy as Aimee when he'd taken her home. A slow smile spread over his face. She was amazingly cute when she was sleepy. And when she'd snuggled next to him . . .

Sitting bolt upright, he pushed that thought out of his

head. "Say it out loud, O'Connell. *I am a photographer. I like my freedom.*"

With a single nod, he went back to listing everywhere he could think of to take photos in the near future. He'd give Aimee the help she needed. Then he'd go to the Sunday lunch at his parents' house to put a cap on the Aimee jewelry store week. Hanging out with the family members who managed to come to that week's lunch, some making a long drive to get there, always helped him. He could start fresh with no more Aimee.

After a quick breakfast of oatmeal and the questionable banana, he checked his gear, stowed it in the trunk, and headed toward the Homer Spit, the opposite direction from Aimee's home.

He left his cottage, drove through downtown Homer, and down the Spit, arriving right on time. With his camera up on a tripod, he watched and waited for the sun to come over the horizon on the bay. When it did, he could see wisps of clouds picking up color as the dawn brought shades of pink and coral to the sky and the water.

He snapped photo after photo, becoming ever more grateful for this place that he had chosen to call home. Even with the leaves gone from the trees, Homer gave him an endless array of photo opportunities. Today's calm water called to him. Maybe he could find someone in the marina who wouldn't mind a passenger later today. He'd love to try for some more whale photos. He loved those and *always* found buyers for them.

With the sun overhead and the early morning's colors

fading, he packed up and headed toward Aimee's house, expecting to get a message from her at any moment asking about her keys, but none came. Maybe she wouldn't realize she didn't have her keys until she stood in front of her store's door and reached for them. Then, panic would ensue.

He parked to the side of her grandparents' large white home. As he walked up to the front door, it opened before he reached it, exactly as it had last night. Aimee's grandmother waited in the doorway. He realized that people inside must hear the crunch of tires on gravel as his vehicle came up their long drive. There weren't any city noises to block that out, nothing but birdsong.

"Are you here to see Aimee again?" She tilted her head and smiled at him. He read too much hope for Aimee and him in her expression.

Jack held up Aimee's keyring. "When I helped her close up last night, I ended up with her keys. I'd like to give them to her."

"I'd like for you to give them to her too, but we have not been able to get her up." Aimee's grandmother cast a worried expression to her right and up. He guessed that was the direction of Aimee's room.

"Is she okay?"

"We believe so. I think it's like jet lag, and she's sleeping off many hours without sleep. We tried nudging her shoulder and even held a steaming cup of coffee—one of her favorite things—under her nose. Neither worked."

He had noticed Aimee's fondness for coffee. Grinning, he held out the keys. "Then I guess I'll just ask you to hand these to her when she gets up."

The older woman stared at the keys with that concerned expression remaining on her face. Then she looked up at him, and a smile started. "Didn't you say that you used to have a jewelry store?"

"Yes."

"And you helped Aimee at her store yesterday, right?"

He hoped this conversation wasn't leading where he thought it was. "Yesterday and before that too."

She smiled widely, again reminding him of Aimee. "Would you do us the great favor of taking care of Aimee's store this morning? I assume that she's going to wake up in an hour or two, and then she can relieve you."

He stared at her, dumbfounded. Before he could stop himself, words tumbled out. "I'd hoped to find a charter today to take me out on the water to try to get more whale photos."

A smug expression crossed her face, like the cat who had caught the canary, and he grew really concerned. "You haven't spent enough time with our granddaughter for her to have talked about her grandparents, have you?"

"It's been all business." He hoped those words would put an end to any hopes her grandparents had for the two of them being anything more than friends.

"We own a fishing charter business. My husband is out on one of our boats right now with a group of passengers. I can trade you the time that you're working for Aimee for free time out on the water."

His jaw dropped. He didn't know anyone around here who owned a boat, so he'd had to pay for the last charter, and they didn't come cheaply. Before he could overthink it, he said, "Deal." Then he felt a moment of guilt. Aimee had already given him some of the labor with his mother's necklace.

She gave a satisfied nod. Then she looked concerned. "I

just remembered that you said you wouldn't remember the alarm code."

He felt a little guilty about that misdirection. "I didn't want her to be concerned about someone who was close to a stranger knowing that much about her business and security. That's why I said *few* would remember. I actually have a hard time forgetting numbers. I also stood beside her when she opened her safe yesterday, so I know those numbers too."

"My goodness! It's a good thing you're on her side."

He laughed. "It probably is. Once she has stopped needing my help, I'll advise her to change her store's alarm code, so that there's never any question about whether or not I was the one who did something. Not that she would ever incorrectly accuse someone of wrongdoing," he rushed to add.

They ended the conversation with Mrs. Jones agreeing to send Aimee to the store once she was up and about. On his drive into town, he wondered how on earth he had gotten himself into this mess. Knowing Adam would be up, he called him.

His brother answered with, "Is anything wrong, Jack?"

"You mean I can't call my brothers without there being something wrong?"

"Of course not. It's that you don't usually call when I'm getting ready to go into school. So I'll ask again, what's wrong?"

That was the problem with close family. They sometimes knew you better than you knew yourself. "Remember the match that Bree set me up with?"

"Of course. Did she turn out to be a chain-smoking nut?"

Jack had to laugh at that. "No. Aimee is better than that. It's just that she owns a jewelry store."

When Jack didn't add any more, his brother asked, "I know that. You still haven't told me what's wrong."

Jack gave a frustrated groan. "*She owns a jewelry store.*" He said every word slowly and deliberately.

"Like I said, I know that. Does it bother you so much that a woman owns a jewelry store? Is that it?"

"Of course not! Women can do anything they want, especially in Alaska. And I know plenty of women who own jewelry stores elsewhere. It's just that I've gotten tangled up in the store. She needed help, and I provided it."

"The Fluffy Syndrome, huh?"

"Fluffy all the way." Jack heard the screech of little girls in the background. That would be his nieces Abbie and Ivy. "Do you need to go?"

"No, Holly's hustling the girls out the door to school right now. The screech was because Chloe bounded over to give them a goodbye kiss as they headed out."

Jack grinned at the idea of the two little girls and the exuberant golden retriever.

"Why don't you explain to me what's going on. I can't help—and my guess is that you called for help—unless I have the whole story."

That made sense. Jack told Adam what had happened from the moment he'd seen the messed-up jewelry display until now.

"I think you've been a good Samaritan. You've done what a lot of people wouldn't, and that isn't bad, Jack. Helping others, both human and small furry creatures, is part of who you are."

"But . . . Fluffy." Jack drove into the small town and slowed down to navigate the somewhat more congested roads.

"We all loved Fluffy. She was a wonderful cat for many years. I know we tease you about her, but it isn't a bad thing that you like to help others as long as you don't get sucked into their trouble."

As Jack parked the SUV about a block from the jewelry store, he realized that what his brother had said was true. He was just helping, and it wasn't costing him anything but time, and it was time that he currently had anyway.

"So tell me about the woman. Aimee Jones sounds pretty nice. Interested?" He could almost see Adam rubbing his hands together with glee. With all but one of his brothers either married or engaged, there were even more people pushing him down the aisle.

If his mother had asked, he would have come up with a glib reply, but this was his brother. "She's not my type, Adam. She's very feminine and girly. I need someone who's willing to go out in the woods and be part of an outdoorsy lifestyle with me as I take my photos. I'd like my special someone to share that life with me at times."

"That sounds silly. Holly looks feminine, but she can also stand in a river and fish beside me."

"Aimee isn't right for me."

"Are you sure?" Jack didn't reply, but he definitely heard disappointment in his brother's voice.

Jack got out of his SUV and started walking down to the store. "I am. I think the biggest thing, anyway, is that I don't want to be tied to someone who has this six-day-a-week commitment to a retail storefront. Adam, she worked thirty-six hours straight, maybe even more than that. I just escaped from a store, and I don't want to go back."

"Now you're talking sense, Jack. I can understand that. The whole pink and feminine thing makes less sense."

He stopped in front of Homer Gems. "I better go now. Oh, and say a quick prayer for me that I do remember the alarm code. Or I may be calling for bail money soon."

Adam chuckled. Then he promised to be at the Sunday lunch but said he thought Holly and the girls would be spending the weekend with her sisters.

Jack quickly entered the numbers into the keypad and breathed a sigh of relief when the red light on the monitor flipped to green. His memory had not failed him. The safe was a different matter because he hadn't personally opened it. He had to rely strictly on his memory from watching, and that was not quite as good. But it would be a strange jewelry store that didn't have wedding rings or a storefront window display, so he hoped he figured it out.

When he pushed on the arm-locking mechanism after using the numbers he remembered, nothing happened. Closing his eyes, he pictured Aimee spinning the dial and opening the safe. When he tried again, this time he was rewarded with the arm swinging down when he pushed on it.

Fifteen minutes later, he had all of the jewelry in the displays where it should be and was standing behind the counter, staring out at his temporary domain. Life had some interesting twists. His mom had said that to him when he was a child. He could still remember the moment. He'd been surprised when he actually liked the art class he'd had to take in junior high. His mother had said, "The unexpected can be much better than the expected. Always leave yourself open, Jack, for good things."

He wasn't sure yet if this was a good thing or not, but he didn't hate it, and that surprised him. Not being responsible for the store was a whole lot nicer than it all being on his shoulders.

He unlocked the front door and went into the back again, taking the box of jobs out of the safe. He set them on her desk and sorted through them, always listening for a ding from the front bell. He chose a re-tipping job that he knew he could easily do.

He sat down, put on his visor, and went to work with the torch and white gold to build up the worn prongs on the setting of a wedding ring's center diamond. Each time the bell chimed, he went out expecting it to be Aimee but found customers instead. He set up an appointment for one of them for that afternoon, assuming that Aimee would have to wake up at some point and come to work.

CHAPTER NINE

$\mathcal{A}$imee opened her eyes and quickly closed them again when the bright sun streaming through the window blinded her. She pulled the covers over her head and turned onto her side to snuggle back into them. Then she realized that there shouldn't be sun streaming onto her when she woke up on a workday morning.

Sitting bolt upright in bed, she glanced around. This was her room at her grandparents' home. She reached for the phone on the nightstand, but it wasn't there. Looking down, she realized that she was still wearing the clothes she'd worn to work two days ago. She slid her feet into the slippers that she'd left there yesterday morning—at least that was a constant—and went into the bathroom.

The clock hanging on the wall normally served to remind her not to take too much time getting ready in the morning. It said 10:15. She had overslept.

Her business was supposed to have opened over an hour ago. She couldn't throw on clothes and run out of here. The face that stared back at her from the mirror not only looked half asleep, but it was topped with stringy hair that hadn't been washed in days. She didn't even want to know how she smelled by this point. By the time she showered and dressed and then got to Homer Gems, it would be close to noon.

Yet one more thing she'd done wrong with her business! At least she'd had Jack to help her. He'd become the shining light in the chaos she called a business. No one could have been more kind. Her heart went pitter-patter just thinking about him. *Just a friend.* She couldn't let her heart rule her head. Besides, this man had made it clear that he was helping a friend. But there was the almost kiss.

Aimee turned on the shower, stripped off, and got in. The feel of the hot water on her started to unwind muscles and finished waking her up. Yesterday afternoon and evening were a vague memory. She'd been working at her bench. And the job had gone well, or at least she thought it had.

And then . . . nothing.

She turned off the water and stared at herself in the mirror as she stepped out. It would take some serious makeup to cover up the exhaustion still showing on her face. She must have slept twelve to fifteen hours. But how had she gotten here?

There was a knock at the bathroom door. She pulled her robe on and said, "Come in."

Her grandmother opened the door and peered around the corner. "I heard you up and about. How are you this morning?"

"I was still wearing yesterday's clothes, but I seem okay. What happened to me?"

Her grandmother watched her as though she was gauging her response to her next words. "Jack brought you home. He carried you into the house because you were sound asleep."

Embarrassment rushed through her. "Carried me? You must mean he helped me in the door, right?" *Please, please, please, let it be that.* It would be too embarrassing for him to have carried her. And to have no memory of those strong arms lifting her up and holding her close to his chest . . . No, she pushed those thoughts out of her head.

Her grandmother looked at her with a combination of pity and amusement. "I'm sorry to say this, Aimee, but you were out cold. He not only carried you into the house from his vehicle, but he set you down in the living room and covered you with the throw."

Her hand flew to her mouth.

"But he did join us for dinner. You don't remember that, either?"

Aimee struggled to recollect anything from the previous evening. "What did we have for dinner? If you tell me, maybe that will jiggle my memory."

"Halibut, potatoes, green beans. Does that do anything for you?"

She nodded slowly. "I do remember that. I seem to remember Jack at the table with us, but that feels like it was a dream."

That speculative glance reappeared. "A good dream or a bad dream?"

Aimee laughed. "Just a dream." But when she thought about it, it did fall more into the category of a good dream than anything else. The clock caught her attention, and she picked up her hair-dryer. "I'd better get to the store, Grandma. I sure hope I didn't lose too much business this morning." She gave a frustrated sigh. "And I still need to finish that ring set."

"Jack opened the store for you this morning."

Aimee set the hair-dryer back down with a thunk. "How did he do that? He had to be able to get in there."

"He brought the keys over this morning. When he got home last night, he found them in his coat pocket. He'd apparently had to lock up the store last night because you couldn't."

Aimee struggled to remember the last half of the previous day. "I hope I didn't botch that entire ring set, Grandma. Every time I think about yesterday afternoon and evening, it's little more than a blur." *Note to self: never try to work two days without sleeping again.* Aimee held up one hand in a *stop* motion. "Hold it, Grandma. I do remember Jack saying that he didn't remember the alarm code."

Her grandmother grinned. "I asked him about that today too. He reminded me that what he'd said was *few* people would remember it. He's one of those few."

So he had opened her store. That was good. She pictured it open, then sighed again. "But there won't be any jewelry in the front window or wedding rings in the wedding case because that's all locked in the safe."

"No, dear. He saw you open the safe yesterday too, and he thought he would remember the combination as well. He apparently has some sort of affinity with numbers and easily remembers them."

"What?! It isn't that I don't appreciate his help. But he's a virtual stranger who has access to everything that is involved with my livelihood."

"He did suggest you have it changed once he was out of the picture."

She had to give him credit for honesty. She reached for the hair-dryer again. "I'd better get a move on." Her grandmother slipped out the door, and Aimee finished getting ready, adding a bit more makeup than her usual mascara, blush, and lip gloss. She grabbed clothes out of her closet with little consideration for what they were. When she checked her appearance in the mirror as she was about to head downstairs, she realized she had paired a red-and-black plaid top with a skirt covered in pink and purple flowers. She ripped the top off and grabbed a solid pink one to put on. She'd been wearing a lot of flowers and pink lately, so she'd need to start mixing that up again.

As she started down the stairs, she reached into her purse for her keys, swishing her hand around inside the big bag and not finding any. Pausing, she looked inside it to check visually. Then she remembered that Jack had her keys. *All* of her keys.

Looking up, she saw her grandmother standing at the bottom of the stairs with her coat on, her purse over her shoulder, and a picnic basket in her hand. "I'm driving you into work today. Your car's apparently parked where you put it Tuesday morning."

Seated next to her grandmother in her sedan, Aimee tried once again to remember the day before. This hadn't been her best start to a day. She felt out of sorts and somewhat disgruntled. She fought against being curt with her words as she asked, "I know you wanted me to sleep longer this morning, but it probably would have been better if you or Grandpa had woken me up." There. She'd said it, and she hadn't been too harsh.

Her grandmother glanced over at Aimee. She drove carefully, with her hands at ten o'clock and two o'clock on the steering wheel as she must have been taught as a young girl. Calmly, Grandma replied, "We tried."

Aimee swallowed a reply that she would probably regret

later and settled into the seat, choosing silence instead. As the minutes passed, she decided to focus on the ring set that she was currently making as she usually would on the way to work. But she couldn't picture what she'd done yesterday afternoon. Her mood turned uglier by the time her grandmother pulled up in front of the store.

"I can't park here, Aimee, so I'll just drop you off. Will we see you for dinner tonight?"

Aimee paused with her hand on the door handle and took a deep breath. Her grandmother didn't deserve a nasty reply. "I guess so. I think that I can finish these rings before dinnertime." As her grandmother started to speak, she added, "Don't worry. I'm not going to spend the night here again. If I need more time, I'll come in early tomorrow morning."

Her grandmother smiled at her.

"I'd better get in there and see what's going on with this stranger who's running my business."

Her grandmother put her hand on Aimee's arm. "Aimee, I don't think you can call Jack a stranger anymore. From everything he's done, I think you'd better call him a *friend* instead."

She wasn't sure how to reply to that, so she just smiled at her grandmother and got out of the car.

Aimee walked in the door just after noon. She was carrying a picnic basket in one hand and wore a grumpy expression on her face.

"Jack! Why didn't you have them wake me up? I have to get those rings done before tomorrow morning."

She plunked the picnic basket down on the counter and headed for the back.

"Didn't you talk to your grandmother this morning?"

"She said they tried to wake me up, but I can't believe they tried very hard."

He raised one eyebrow. "Aimee, she said that she tried waving coffee under your nose. You didn't budge."

She stopped. "They tried coffee? I always get up for the smell of coffee." She made a sound between a sigh and a groan. "Even though I've never had anyone wave some under my nose while I was sound asleep. I think I might owe Grandma an apology."

"Were you cranky this morning?"

She pursed her lips and waved a hand from side to side. "More than she deserved. My first thought when I opened my eyes was that I had to get to work. My second thought was that I needed a shower."

He laughed. "I think I'm glad you had that second thought."

"You should be. It had been a while since I'd taken one, and I've been working pretty hard. Making jewelry doesn't look like it's physical work—"

"I know, but sometimes you're throwing your whole body into it. You're hammering, or you're cutting something with a graver, and then there's always the torch, which is heat."

She looked at him and smiled. "I haven't had anybody who understood my work since I left London."

"London, England?"

"Yes, I studied with a master jeweler there for three years. Every chance I got, though, I came back to Homer to spend time with Grandma and Grandpa. My parents divorced when I was a kid and have new families now, so being with my grandparents always felt more like home. By the time my apprenticeship was over, I knew this was where I wanted to be."

He now understood her high skill level. She wasn't just a jeweler who had taken a few classes, she was an artisan.

She headed toward the back. "Grandma packed up something for lunch. You're welcome to eat it. Or you can leave now if you want, Jack. I appreciate what you did very much, but I think I can manage the store and the jewelry work the rest of the afternoon."

As she disappeared around the corner to her bench, the door chimed, and two women walked in. He wondered if he should help them, but Aimee came out and greeted them. He grabbed the picnic basket and headed to the back. It had been a long time since his skimpy breakfast, so he'd take advantage of this homemade food, and then he'd be on his way. Now he had the fishing charter with her grandfather to look forward to.

He finished a roast beef sandwich, an apple, and a cranberry-apple muffin, and Aimee still hadn't returned to the back. He sat back to relax for a few minutes and then heard the door chime as someone left.

A few seconds later, Aimee came into the back room and stared at him with weary eyes. "Jack, I think my arrogance has gotten away with me. Is there any way that you can help me out the rest of today so that I can finish these rings? I have a lot of other jobs that are due, but nothing is more important than these."

"I can do that. Under one condition."

She looked at him.

"Can I have dinner with your grandmother and grandfather again?"

She grinned and laughed. "Grandma's a good cook, isn't she?"

"Second only to my mother. I've been eating my bachelor-on-the-go food for too long. My mom usually cooks for the family every Saturday, but this week it's Sunday. I have that to look forward to three days from now, but otherwise not so good."

As they settled into work, her at her workbench and him beside her at the second bench, she asked, "How many brothers and sisters do you have?"

"Four brothers. And we all live within a few hours of our parents now."

"That's nice. My mother is in Reno. She remarried and had one child who is ten years younger than me. My dad is in Boston and has three kids I've only met a couple of times."

Jack pulled a ring sizing job out of the box and grimaced. It was the oldest job and needed to be done, but he hated ring sizing. "Your grandparents are special people."

She turned the ring she worked on from side to side in her hands. "They are. They treat all of their grandchildren as special—when they visit, which isn't too often—but I'm oldest and seem to have a different relationship with them." With that, she shifted into work mode and didn't say anything more.

He slid the ring onto the long ring mandrel to compare it to the sizes marked by lines on the long tool, saw that it needed to go down a full size to be what the envelope said, then chose a place to cut the metal and began sawing.

In between customers, they sat side by side, working. He managed to finish all of the jobs that weren't design related, with only a question now and then to make sure he understood her usual procedure.

Just after 5:00 p.m., Aimee pushed back from her chair, stood up, and spun in a circle with her hands in the air exactly as he'd seen the first moment he walked in the door. She let out a whoop. "It is *done*. The whole project is done! Now I just have to pray they don't have any last-minute changes." She spun one more time, then stopped and stared at him, turning bright red. "Oh, my goodness! I can't believe I just did that in front of someone!"

He laughed so hard that he doubled over and gasped for air. "Aimee, I thought you were a nut the first time I saw you do that. But now that I know you, well, I still think you're a little nutty, but in a really good way."

She reached out and swatted at his arm. "Thank you very much. I always reserve my happy dances for times when I'm alone. But this was so exciting that I got carried away." She stretched to her right, her left, then leaned over and let her arms dangle. "I am so glad this job is done. My back is glad it's done too." Standing upright, she added, "And I can't even begin to thank you for not only waiting on my customers but for finishing up so many of these little jobs. I feel like I can breathe again."

She checked the time. "I'm ready to shut this place down for the day. That will be about twenty minutes before my hours say I close, but I don't care."

He turned off the torch and tidied up the desk, knowing he wouldn't be here again. They worked together to take the jewelry out of the cases, then he waited for her out front while she stowed it in the safe. When she came out, he reached in his pocket and pulled out the keys. "I believe you want these."

"Yes, I do. But if you hadn't had them, my store would

have been closed for half of the day. I can't thank you enough."

Before he'd given it any thought, he said, "Would you like to go to dinner with me tonight?"

She looked at him and cocked her head to the side, as though she was evaluating whether or not she should have anything more to do with him. "Knowing my grandmother, she has a great meal waiting at home, and there's plenty. Would you like to have one of those homemade meals tonight?"

It wasn't quite as good as having dinner alone with Aimee, and he did not even want to consider for a second why he would rather do that, but her family was very welcoming. "I would love to. If you want to head over to the door, I'll take care of the alarm."

Aimee raised one eyebrow, then shrugged and did as he'd said. "Why not?"

They went opposite directions to their vehicles when they left the store. Jack looked forward to seeing Aimee again soon. He enjoyed her smile, just being around her. He pushed away his concern at those thoughts. He'd only agreed to dinner.

·

CHAPTER TEN

*W*ith every minute that passed during her drive home, Aimee wondered more and more what she had been thinking. Sure, Jack wasn't the man she'd thought he was. He'd started out as the engaged jerk who'd asked her out. But he was honorable. He had helped her beyond what anyone had any reason to do. The problem was that her heart did funny things when he was near. She'd had to focus intently on her work to forget he sat close by today.

When she pulled into the driveway, she found that he'd beat her there, probably because he'd had a shorter walk to his vehicle. She climbed out of her car, expecting to find him in his, but he'd already gone inside. From the little she remembered from the night before, Jack and her grandparents had become buddies in a short amount of time.

As they ate some sort of chicken and noodle casserole her grandmother had made and drank glasses of iced tea, her grandparents questioned him about his life.

"I have four brothers," Jack explained. "They live between here and Palmer. My parents are in Kenai."

Her grandfather asked, "Where are you living while you're here? I believe you mentioned it was a short-term rental."

"Yes, sir. Someone who works at Cinnamon Bakery owns it, and they're letting me stay there week to week, but I'd really like to find something more permanent."

The older man said, "The owners are probably Mandy's parents. Mandy's mother helps out sometimes, and I know they own a rental. But I would expect that there are a lot of rentals this time of year. The tourist season is all but over now."

Jack scooped another serving of the casserole onto his plate. "That may well be true, but I want something with a view. I want to be able to step out my door and see natural beauty, and that's not something I'm willing to give up on. I have found a couple of places with a great view, but that I wouldn't have chosen as home."

Aimee's grandfather chuckled. "I've seen some of those places. We had someone working for us one summer, and he rented a place that he said had a solid roof and an indoor bathroom, but that's about all he could say that would recommend it."

Jack grinned. "That just about sums it up for some of them. I'm still holding out hope, though."

Aimee's grandfather smiled at his wife. "This is a delicious meal, Terri."

She laughed. "He says that every night."

"It's true every night. You've settled on Homer, Jack?"

Jack took a sip of his tea. "I do want to make Homer my home."

The older man glanced from him to Aimee and back to him, then he turned and looked at his wife. She gave a slow nod as though she had agreed to some unspoken question. When they'd finished, he stood and said, "We may have a place for you."

Aimee gasped.

Jack looked at Aimee and shrugged. "Do you know what they're talking about?"

"I believe I do." She looked at her grandparents. "Do you really want to do this? We just met him."

Her grandmother said, "Aimee girl, this man has done more for you in one week than a lot of people do for each other in decades. I think we can trust him. Besides, we used to have complete strangers here."

Jack felt like he'd entered a different dimension. Why did he always get this *Alice in Wonderland* sensation when he was with these people? "I'm sure I'll find something—"

Her grandfather held up his hand. "Let us show you this cabin before you make any decisions."

They walked out the front door of the house, then turned to the left, the opposite direction from the driveway. The breathtaking view out toward the bay kept catching Jack's attention.

When they neared it, he saw that what they'd called a cabin was actually a small, white, clapboard cottage, one of half a dozen scattered around that side of the property. It did look freshly painted, and it had a good roof on it, so it surpassed most of the potential rentals he'd looked at.

"Why are there so many of these buildings? Are they workshops or storage?"

Aimee's grandfather answered. "When we bought the property, these were rental cabins. The previous owner had built them, and guests could come and stay here overnight. Fifty years ago, there were a lot fewer hotel and motel options, and most of them, with the notable exception of the hotel at the very end of the Spit, didn't have a view like this. We rented them out for the first five or so years that we lived here. It helped us get ahead financially as we built the fishing charter business."

Aimee's grandmother picked up the conversation. "One day, I looked at Carson across the breakfast table, and I said, 'I don't want to clean anybody else's toilets anymore.'"

Her grandfather grinned. "Not your usual breakfast conversation."

Jack chuckled. "No, sir. It isn't. But it does get the point across."

"Yes, it did, son. We finished out our obligations to people who had already booked for that year and then took them off the market. Now it's just family and friends who stay. But the last time we had done any renovations, beyond a coat of paint on the outside to protect them from the elements, was about twenty years ago."

As they drew closer to the cottage, Jack could tell it had been well cared for. He looked to his right and saw that it held that same view as the main house because it was the cabin that was to the front of the property. The others might have an adequate view but nothing like this.

He'd check it out to be polite, but there was no way he would ever want to live this close to Aimee Jones. He enjoyed her company too much to avoid her and did not want a close relationship with someone he couldn't have a real future with.

As they stepped up to the door, her grandfather added, "When we knew that our Aimee girl had decided to move to Homer instead of living near one of her parents or some other place on the planet like London," he gave Aimee a glare that said he had not enjoyed the years when she was on the other side of the Atlantic, "we decided to fix this unit up for her. We thought she deserved privacy when she was here. We know that eventually she'll get her own place, but we've always loved having her close."

Aimee reached for the doorknob. "But I enjoy being around Grandma and Grandpa so much that I didn't want to be in a separate cabin. I'm happy to have my old room in the house."

Her grandmother said, "We decorated this cabin in a way that we thought our Aimee would enjoy."

Jack had a hard time not rolling his eyes. The rustic bench outside didn't have that feeling, but he'd bet this would be decorated very similarly to Mom's shabby chic guest room which had flowers everywhere. No matter how awesome the view, he had to stay firm. He just wasn't the kind of guy who could live just anywhere. Sure, he could live in a tent for a week at a time, but when he came back to town, he wanted to feel at home. Pink never did that for him.

Aimee turned the knob and pushed the door open.

He stepped into the cottage, expecting to hate what he saw, but instead he found a tiny living area, a small kitchen and a table for two on the left, and a doorway to the right where he could see a small bedroom, which looked to have a double bed in it.

The biggest surprise was that it wasn't pink. "It's beautiful." Yellow and sapphire blue—the same colors he'd seen in her bedroom—and green were the theme. The wall behind the small sofa was clad in rough-hewn wood in an almost driftwood color. The kitchen counters were white. "May I?" He pointed toward the bedroom

Aimee's grandmother answered. "Of course. The bathroom is through the bedroom. That would make it a little inconvenient if you had guests, but it worked fine as an overnight rental."

The bedroom actually held a queen-size bed, much better for his six-foot frame than the double he'd expected. The design aesthetic continued through there. The headboard was again of that driftwood-colored wood. One detail they must have added for Aimee was a shelf filled with books. He stepped closer to see if he found any he'd enjoy. Every one of them was a romance novel. Definitely not his choice.

He peered into the bathroom. It was compact but had a nice stand-up shower, a vanity with a sink, and a toilet, with the tile and paint all in neutral colors with the same white countertops as the kitchen.

He spun on his heels and hurried out to the living area. "How much do you want for this per month?"

They quoted him a figure that was much less than he'd expected to have to pay.

"Sold." And then he saw Aimee's expression. He could tell that she was less than pleased to have him as basically a neighbor.

"But don't worry about me. I can take care of myself, and I don't expect to be included in any family functions."

Aimee nodded her head vigorously. She looked at her grandmother and grandfather as if hoping they would second that notion.

"Jack, you're welcome anytime you'd like to stop in for dinner. Maybe you could show us some of the pictures you've been taking next time."

Aimee's shoulders slumped. Did she not want someone to live on the property, or was it just him? And should he respect her wishes and rescind his acceptance of the rental?

He wandered over to the window in the living room, a wide one that took up a big section of the wall but was divided into small windows with mullions in between, which added to the charm of the cottage.

The view out the windows had him inhale sharply. He'd looked at so many properties as he tried to find a permanent place to live, and this one fit everything he'd been asking for. It was an answer to prayer. He hoped that Aimee wouldn't be too upset by him being nearby and that they could become friends.

"When can I move in?"

Her grandfather answered. "It's yours, son. Move in anytime you like and bring the check over the next time you stop by for dinner." At that moment, her grandfather looked from Jack to Aimee and smiled.

Okay. That put a new spin on things. They liked him enough to rent to him, that was clear, but it might also be that they'd put him nearby because he was a strong candidate for grandson-in-law. He'd noticed their matchmaking in the past but wished it didn't extend so far that they'd rented to him to match them up. Turning back toward the window, he knew that he could defend himself against matchmaking. This was going to be his home for a while.

Jack followed Aimee and her grandparents back to the main house.

Back inside, they sat in the living room, and her grandmother brought slices of apple pie she'd made earlier that day. "I've warmed this up in the oven so that it could take the chill off of us after being outside." She shivered. "It does get cool in the evenings this time of year, doesn't it?"

Jack accepted a piece of pie from her. He glanced over at

Aimee where she sat in that same chair across from him. Frowning.

Her grandfather asked her, "How is that big project going, my girl?"

She brightened up. "I finished it, Grandpa. I hope they love it. It's exactly what they asked for, and I did not deviate from the original drawings."

"Then I'm sure they'll love it. Everyone loves what you make."

She seemed to be thinking. "So far, so good. And Jack helped me a lot by getting many of the small jobs taken care of. Once they've picked up the rings tomorrow morning, I will truly feel like a burden has lifted off of my shoulders."

Her grandfather gave Jack an admiring glance. That gave the older man one more reason for him to trust him as a future family member. "Jack, you used to have a jewelry store. Did you work this hard?"

He considered how to answer that. He didn't want to annoy Aimee, but he felt deep in his heart that she might need some help. "Sometimes. I don't have Aimee's gift at the bench, though. My work has fewer frills. But I worked six days a week for years, and it was almost impossible to get away. At least I thought it was impossible. I now realize that I should have taken off a day now and then or even a half a day."

He took another bite of the warm pie before continuing. "I was in Fairbanks, so I probably could have closed for half of January, and nobody would have missed it. There are few tourists right after Christmas, and it's usually bitterly cold."

The woman smiled at him and then looked at her granddaughter. "Are you going to take some time off soon, Aimee?"

Aimee's frown turned into a scowl, and she glared at Jack. It looked like he might have reopened a can of worms. "I'm building my business, Grandma. I hope to be able to have some help in the future and then maybe take some time off."

Jack looked at her and noticed that the dark circles under her eyes remained. "Maybe you could leave work at lunchtime tomorrow and have some fun for a while."

He wouldn't have thought it was possible a moment ago, but the scowl deepened, and the glare became more fierce. "You should understand, Jack. You owned a business. I have to take care of it first."

He stood. "I don't want to upset you, but you actually have to take care of yourself first. You need to relax. And as long as you put a sign on your door that you'll be back the next day, in a town this size I'm sure you'll be absolutely fine, and you won't lose business."

Aimee's brow furrowed as she seemed to try to sort out what he had said.

Her grandfather said, "I agree."

"Grandpa, you're the worst one to agree. You work hard all the time every day of the week."

He held up one finger. "But it's only for one season. The rest of the year, when it's not the height of tourist and fishing season, I only work a couple of days a week. Some of my boats don't go out at all. Balance, my girl, balance."

She reached up and rubbed her forehead.

He certainly didn't want to be the cause of a headache. "I'll move into the cottage within the next couple of days." He gave a wave and started for the door.

Aimee said, "Wait a minute, Jack." He turned toward her. "I feel like everyone has ganged up on me. But I know that I haven't recovered from working so many hours straight."

She turned toward her grandfather. "Grandpa, if you want to take Jack out on your boat tomorrow, I'll leave the store early and take a break and come with you. It's been a long time since I've been out on the saltwater."

Her grandfather clapped his hands. "That's my girl. That's smart, and we raised you to be smart."

She looked toward Jack. He wondered why on earth she wanted him along for the ride. "Then we can kill two birds with one stone. Jack gets his charter, and I take my afternoon off. Then everyone should be happy, and we're even, right?" She looked around the room at the three people in it.

Her grandparents wore gleeful expressions. Even Aimee appeared happy. She either wanted to spend time with him, which came as a surprise, or wanted to pay him back quickly for everything he had done. That made the most sense.

Jack left. As he drove away, he continued wondering what he had gotten himself into. He had that feeling every time he came in contact with these people, and now he'd be living next door. But this rental was far above any other that he'd seen, and the price was much below, so he would be a fool not to take it. And no one had ever called Jack O'Connell a fool.

CHAPTER ELEVEN

*a*fter Jack left, Aimee's grandfather said to her, "I didn't want to mention this with Jack here because he doesn't know you as I do, but I'm going to have you take him out on the boat tomorrow. Your grandmother promised him a day on the water for helping you today, and I need to see to the engine repair on one of the other boats. You're as good on the ocean as many of my captains, better than some."

Her grandfather's words were true. She'd been here every summer for most of her life and piloted his boats alone many times, but doing this would mean she was completely alone on the bay for hours with Jack O'Connell, and that was not a place she wanted to be.

"Grandpa, it's been a while since I've taken one your boats out. Wouldn't it be better if you did it?"

He gave her what she'd always called the Grandpa Stare when she was little. It was somehow all-knowing. "I thought you might say that, so I'm going to take you out for about an hour first to put you through the paces, and then you're on your own. Fair enough?" With that, he stood, turned to his wife, and said, "I'm going to bed earlier than normal to read. Aimee and I will have an early start in the morning."

With that, both he and her grandmother left, her grandmother looking over her shoulder as they walked away to say, "I hope you sleep well tonight, dear. I'll have a good breakfast waiting for you in the morning."

Aimee gave a small wave to her, and her grandma smiled. They'd managed to get her to do exactly what they wanted.

As soon as she got up to her room, Aimee called Molly. "Would you like to go out on one of Grandpa's boats tomorrow?"

"You know I can't get away from the bakery."

"It would be after lunch. Could your mom fill in for you for the afternoon?"

"Let me double-check with her. I know I don't have any birthday cakes to make or any events that I'm catering tomorrow. I'll call you right back."

Aimee sat on the edge of the bed and tapped her fingers on her nightstand. She and Jack had been set up by her grandparents, and she really didn't want to be alone with him for hours with no customers or work to focus on.

Molly called back. "Mom's on board with it. I'm pretty excited about this. It's been a while since I went out with your grandfather. There were two openings on one of his fishing charters?"

"Would it upset you if I told you that it wasn't Grandpa at the helm but me?"

Her friend laughed. "I've been out on the water with you so many times that it doesn't bother me in the slightest."

"Which boat?"

"The Terri Marie."

"That's my favorite. I'll meet you down there tomorrow. Bye."

Problem solved. Now she just had to figure out where they would go, a trip that would be grand enough to repay Jack for everything he'd done for her. The labor for his mother's necklace wasn't nearly enough payment. Him being there had taught her that she did need help in the store, but it didn't change the fact that she couldn't pay for it yet. Maybe when Christmastime came, she could at least find a college student home for break to help out.

CHAPTER TWELVE

*J*ack felt like beating his head against the wall.
Matchmakers, matchmakers, everywhere were
matchmakers. And now he was stuck spending
the afternoon with Aimee, which should be a fabulous free
afternoon out on the water so that he could take photos.
Sure, her grandfather would be there, but her grandfather
would be piloting the boat and would probably find some
way to stay busy and separate from them the entire time. He
could just envision it right now, her grandfather saying
something like, "You kids go have fun. Relax in the back and
enjoy the view."

He paced around his cottage. To make matters worse, he
was now, or at least he would be in a few days, living next
door. Pausing, he struggled to relax. He could handle that. He
would come and go on his own terms, and Aimee being there
would not matter very much. At least he hoped it wouldn't.
There was still tomorrow, though.

Then a brilliant idea came to him. He grabbed his phone
and pushed the speed dial for his brother Andy.

Andy answered. "Hey, bro, how are things in Homer? I've been meaning to call you, but I figured I'd just stop by once you got your permanent digs there."

"Are you busy with work?"

"I finally got caught up after all that time working on Maddie's house. Right now, I was just thinking about a new project that I've acquired. Creative time if you will."

His oldest brother, Mark, had called in all hands to help finish Maddie's house when her contractor had run out on her. They'd all grown up with Maddie living down the street from them in Juneau, so they'd been happy to help.

Jack felt guilty for asking Andy to help him out after he'd just helped Mark. But only for a second. "Andy, would you like to go out on a boat tomorrow on Kachemak Bay? Maybe the ocean beyond it too. I'm not sure exactly where we're going."

His brother groaned. "You know my soft spot for the water. I just don't know if I can, though."

An afternoon alone with Aimee loomed in front of him.

"This isn't going to be some small dinghy bobbing around on the big water, is it?" Andy asked suspiciously.

Jack laughed. "Would I do that to you?"

"You would and did."

"Hey, it wasn't a dinghy."

"You're right. It wasn't a dinghy. It was an old wooden boat that leaked."

Jack could picture the old boat with worn paint and a barely legible name. He'd bought it with earnings from his first job. "When you're right, you're right. We had a lot of fun with it that first day, didn't we?"

"I'm just grateful that we did not try to open the hatch into the hold of the boat until we were near shore. Bailing the water out then wasn't anywhere near as terrifying as it would have been if we'd been further out."

Jack grinned. "In answer to your question, no, this is a commercial boat that regularly takes passengers out. I helped someone out, and this is their thanks."

"An afternoon in the Homer area on a commercial boat? Count me in. I'll catch up on work later. What time should I meet you and where? And do you have a place for me to sleep?"

"The couch is comfortable." Jack gave his brother directions to his home, then followed up with a text that had the actual address, which he wasn't sure would help since he was in a small house next to a larger one at the same address.

Andy arrived on time, and they drove to the harbor in his pickup. They were getting out of his truck as Molly exited her vehicle. "Are you delivering something wonderful to a boat down here?" He turned toward his brother. "Molly owns Cinnamon Bakery. They make the best cinnamon rolls that you have ever had in your life. And the coffee's excellent too."

His brother gave Molly an interested glance. "I'll definitely have to stop by while I'm here."

Molly blushed, and he wondered if he'd just started something with his brother and the pretty bakery owner. But Molly wasn't unlike Andy in a way that might be a permanent roadblock. His brother had a house on a lake over an hour away, one that he'd had built to his exact specifications and had a hand in making. He didn't see his brother moving to Homer anytime soon, and Molly was stuck here because of her business.

"I'm going to one of the Jones's boats." She reached into her car and brought out a box and carafe, what he hoped was a delivery to the boat he'd be on.

Jack asked, "Coffee?"

She nodded but gave him a puzzled expression.

"I assume all of their boats are moored in the same area, so we're going the same direction."

Molly clearly knew her way around the harbor, so she led the way.

Jack glanced around as they stepped onto the dock. "I'm glad that you came because I wouldn't have known how to get to the boat without calling Aimee for more directions."

"It's pretty straightforward. Did you hire Molly's grandfather to take you out for the afternoon to go fishing?"

"No. He's taking me out this afternoon so that I can take some photos." Jack added, "And Aimee."

Molly stopped in her tracks and turned toward him. "But I'm going out on a boat with Aimee this afternoon."

He could tell when she figured out what was happening, and he was glad someone understood the situation.

She laughed. "Aimee asked if I wanted to go out on the boat. And you asked your brother."

Andy said, "You both found someone to foil her grandfather's matchmaking plans for the two of you."

Molly grinned. "I'd like to be there when her grandparents find out." She pointed to a large white boat with the name *Terri Marie* on the side. Jack knew Terri was Aimee's grandmother's name, so he assumed the boat was named for her.

As they reached it, he could see Aimee standing on board,

but no one else. Her grandfather must have stepped away for a few minutes. Aimee was wearing a red sweater over jeans and no pink in sight.

Molly said, "It'll be the four of us today, then."

Jack turned toward her. "Well, five. It will be the four of us and Aimee's grandfather."

Molly wore a confused expression. "Aimee called me last night and told me that she was piloting today. It's just the four of us."

Jack swiveled slowly and looked up at the woman in front of him. She was the finest jeweler he'd ever worked with, but that didn't mean she knew anything about piloting a boat.

His brother expressed his sentiments. "I may need to get some work done today after all."

"What a bunch of wimps. Aimee knows as much about being on a boat as she does about making jewelry. She grew up working in this business." Molly started to board the boat, leaving the two men behind.

Andy said, "I guess she told us off. Are you going, bro?"

Jack looked at the boat in front of him. It was big and fine, and he wasn't going to turn this down. If Molly said that Aimee knew how to pilot this boat and her grandfather had been willing to let her take out something that was worth a considerable amount of money, not to mention his grand-daughter's life, then it would be okay with him.

Aimee watched Jack and Molly as they boarded the boat with another man. Had Jack decided that he could invite a group?

He stopped and stared at her. His didn't seem filled with glee at seeing her on board. "Aimee Jones, I'd like for you to meet my brother Andy. He and I have always enjoyed being out on the water together. We grew up in Juneau, so we had many afternoons on the saltwater."

She extended her hand. "I'm pleased to meet you, Andy." She could see vague similarities between the two men, but their hair color was somewhat different. Andy's had more of a reddish tint to it, and that made her wonder what Jack's other brothers looked like. Pulling herself together, she said, "Everyone ready to go?" She put on her best confident smile.

Jack spoke with less confidence than she was used to. "I think so. Where are we going?"

She pointed across the bay.

"I know that the massive Kachemak Bay State Park is over there. This is an area I've wanted to explore. Thank you!"

"We still have enough daylight this time of year to take the trip in the afternoon without being concerned about it turning dark before we can get back. And the weather's supposed to be on our side. After the boat ride, I thought we'd go to dinner in Homer. That should pay Jack back for his help." She owed him much more, but he looked happy with her proposal.

Andy spoke up first. "That sounds perfect to me. Do we need to make reservations at the restaurant?"

Aimee was quite glad that her grandmother had suggested that at breakfast. "It's taken care of." Then she frowned. "Well, it's taken care of for three people, but I can't imagine that they have a table that only seats three and not four. I'll call to add you on, Andy."

She walked away to do that. When she returned, she said, "I'm glad we discussed it while we were here, and there was still cell service. I don't know if we'll have any reception where we're going."

Jack laughed. "To my knowledge, there isn't anything in the park except for nature, is there?"

"The place we're going isn't on Grandpa's standard fishing pattern, but we used to go there fairly often as a family. It's only been a park for about fifty years. People lived there before that, so there are home sites, but not much of what you'd call a road—at least none that go far or connect to the outside world."

"Growing up in Homer, it was always one of my favorite places," Molly said. "There are lots of hiking trails. I've kayaked through the bays and watched wildlife. You'll probably get plenty of photos of bald eagles, Jack."

He grinned. "I doubt we'll find a whole lot of people there on a mid-September afternoon. This is great."

It made Aimee's heart happy that Jack loved her idea.

Jack carefully watched Aimee as she started the boat and maneuvered them out of their slip. She moved with complete confidence. When her actions proved she'd done this many times in the past, he relaxed and got his cameras out. They motored across the saltwater, and he kept his eyes out for whales or anything else interesting.

They all crowded around Aimee as she piloted them across the bay.

He said, "You pointed toward the state park, but that covers hundreds of thousands of acres. Do you have a specific destination?"

She glanced over at Jack and grinned. "I do."

"And?" He drew the word out.

She just smiled, and they kept cutting through the water in the boat. The water wasn't flat today, but it wasn't choppy either. It was a beautiful day to be out there. "We *are* going to the park, but we have one stop along the way."

As they continued across the water, a small rocky island came into focus. His jaw dropped. "Gull Island?"

She grinned and nodded.

Andy asked, "Is that good? It seems like it's something good."

Molly replied, "Every year until right about now, tens of thousands of birds nest on this tiny rock island. My favorites are the puffins with their orange beaks and black and white bodies, but there are lots and lots of birds there."

"And we get to walk among them?"

Molly shook her head. "No. The state awarded the island to an Alaska Native group, and they closed it to people walking on it. I 100 percent support that. It's a tiny island, and I'm glad the birds aren't being disturbed."

As they neared the island, she cut the throttle, and they bobbed in the water. The slightly overcast sky with pockets of blue peering through was typical for the weather here. As Jack raised his camera, the sun broke through between two clouds and shot rays of sunlight toward the earth. He snapped photos as it happened, catching every moment. And then it was gone.

His brother stood next to him. "Wow, that was something."

Jack switched to his other camera, focused on the birds, and then suddenly, a bald eagle swooped down from overhead, and thousands of birds took flight. He wished he was recording the sound because the cry of the birds and ruffle of wings was almost deafening. He snapped photo after photo, focusing on one place, and then another, and up into the sky. When the birds settled back down, he let the camera drop so it hung around his neck. He'd just witnessed a miracle. "Thank you, Aimee," he said in a low voice. Taking a deep breath, he composed himself, and then he smiled and looked around. "We can go home now."

Aimee said, "But wait, there's more!"

They all chuckled as she gave the boat power. Once they were away from the island, she opened up the throttle, and they zoomed toward land.

"I know I'll be able to sell some of those photos. And there could be an award winner in there."

Aimee said, "I'm glad it turned out so well. Let's hope that the rest of the day goes equally well for you."

"Hey, what about us? Don't we get any fun back here?" Molly asked.

Aimee said, "Are you enjoying the view and being out on the water? And it's free?"

Molly held up one hand. "Okay. You're right. It's absolutely beautiful out here. I'm so glad it's not choppy. I enjoy being out on the water most times, but I don't like it when it feels like I'm surfing in a boat."

Andy said, "Growing up on the water, we've been out many times when the weather suddenly turned nasty. Boy, do we have stories we could tell you."

When they started to enter a bay, Molly said, "Halibut Cove? I know you made reservations in Homer, but maybe we could change them and eat dinner here?"

Aimee slowed as they passed an area with houses. "The fancy restaurant there is closed by this time of year. I've only eaten there once, but it's a fabulous place."

Andy said, "This area reminds me a little of places near Juneau we explored as kids. Except that here we aren't far from roads that connect you to the rest of the world."

Jack agreed. "I wouldn't trade where we grew up for another place, but I had to agree with Mom and Dad when they decided they wanted to go somewhere where you could drive out and not be limited to air and water transportation."

"It is an odd thing to have a state capital that you can't drive to, isn't it?" Molly agreed.

Jack looked at what appeared to be a community. "I didn't expect more than a few houses. How can they live inside a park?"

"It's been a state park for about fifty years. I guess these home sites are from before that. Or maybe there was some way that they acquired state land. I've never asked. They even have a post office, one of the only *floating* post offices." As they motored past the settled area of Halibut Cove and into more of a wilderness area, Jack marveled at this day that he had received. This gift from Aimee. He would gladly spend a couple more days in her jewelry store to do this again. Not that he'd initially helped her because he'd expected to get anything back, but the reward was far greater than the effort he had expended.

Andy pointed, and Jack lifted his camera toward the otters that his brother had spotted off the side of the boat. Two of them splashed in the water and floated on their backs. Off to the side on a rocky beach, he saw a bald eagle landing next to many others. "The beach is covered with bald eagles." He took photos as they motored by.

As they puttered through the cove, Molly asked, "Are we going into Halibut Cove Lagoon?"

Aimee nodded. "I was thinking of the best places to go for

a short trip. I thought we could get out there and walk a short distance up China Poot trail to First Lake."

Jack turned toward her. "What's the name of the lake?"

Molly answered. "First Lake. That's the official name. I wish that the person who named it had been more creative." As they started around the bend, Molly looked concerned.

"What's wrong, Molly?" Jack asked.

"I was almost grounded in a boat here once when a group of us came, probably before we should have been out on our own on this big body of water. Sections of the lagoon aren't passable unless it's high tide."

Aimee said, "Never fear, my friend. I checked the tide schedule. We are riding in with the tide today, and we'll be able to get back out before it's too low."

Molly breathed a sigh of relief, but she held her shoulders tense as they rounded the bend and went down a narrow body of water. Jack could see a dock at the end. Aimee expertly cruised up to it and stopped the engine. He never should have doubted her abilities. He'd played around in boats from an early age, but he didn't have her skill level. A master jeweler *and* someone able to run a charter business. That was an interesting combination.

As he stepped out on the dock, Jack noticed movement in the woods, and he held out his hand to stop the others from getting out. "Don't move. I think I just saw something large and furry over there."

CHAPTER THIRTEEN

$\mathcal{J}$ack stood still, but was ready to leap for the ladder if he had to.

Halfway down the ladder, Aimee froze.

There were sounds of brush crunching, and then a black bear appeared on the shore. Jack knew he could get out of the way in a hurry, but he had a feeling that the bear wasn't there for them, he was just there. A couple of minutes later, the bear wandered off down the shore and up into the woods again, and Jack heard an audible sigh of relief from the three people in the boat.

Andy asked, "Do we go on the hike or not?"

"The trail starts there." Aimee held onto the ladder with one hand and pointed to their right, the opposite direction from the one the bear had chosen.

Jack answered, "I can easily be thrilled with the photos I've already taken. On the other hand, the bear's gone. You know how it is in Alaska." He shrugged.

Molly said, "We coexist with the big animals. It wouldn't bother me as much if it was a moose because when they're gone, they're gone. A bear . . ." She waved her hand from side to side.

They all got out onto the dock and waited. There was no sign of any other big animals or humans.

Finally, Molly said, "I say we take the hike. Did you bring pepper spray, Aimee?"

Aimee reached into her jacket pocket and held up a spray bottle.

"Ever-prepared Aimee. That's what we used to call her. She spent almost every summer in Homer growing up, and she always seemed to have what we needed for our adventures."

Aimee giggled. Jack had never seen her like that, but he could now see the teenager that she must have been when she and Molly met. "Of course, it didn't hurt that my grandfather had boats, and there's a lot of water to cross."

"True. We had many adventures courtesy of your grandfather."

Their captain started walking. "The bear is long gone, and I'm ready for a hike. We need to get this thing done, so we can ride the tide out of here. Agreed?"

As they started for where the trailhead must be, all he saw were trees and brush. Jack asked, "Where is the trail?"

Aimee said, "It's gotten somewhat overgrown. But I've been here enough times that I should be able to pick my way through the brush to find it, and I think it'll get clearer once we're away from the shore. It probably wouldn't have been passable in the middle of the summer, but the fall frost has killed some of the summer vegetation."

They wound their way through the brush near the shore. As she'd predicted, it got better. They must have walked a mile with trees on either side before they came upon a small lake off to the right.

Jack raised his camera. "First Lake is beautiful." He snapped photos as birds swooped and ducks landed on the water. A sense of calm came over him when Aimee stepped up beside him, and they both looked out at the scene together. He was ashamed to realize that he'd made snap judgments about her, expecting a feminine woman to hate the outdoors. She'd been beside him and ahead of him on this trail the whole way.

He reached out and held her hand, and a sense of rightness fell over him, but he let go. He shouldn't have done that when he knew there was no way they could have a future together. Today was a short break from the business she owned, and that gave her little free time for a life he could share with her. That thought caused him more pain than it should have for the friend she was. "Shouldn't we be going back, Aimee?"

The smile she'd had turned to a frown as she looked up at him and then stepped back. After a pause, she said, "You're absolutely right." She checked her watch. "We've been here quite a while. Let's hustle on back to the boat and get out of here so that we don't freak Molly out."

"Good plan." Molly led them on their way back to the boat.

They puttered out of the lagoon and through the bay, and then Aimee opened up the throttle to quickly eat up the miles between them and the Homer harbor. He wished he could capture today forever and hold it close to him. His heart had gotten involved with Aimee Jones. And there was absolutely nothing that could come of it. He had to pretend that it hadn't happened.

Aimee took the boat into its slip in the harbor. When she stopped, they got out, promising to meet at the restaurant.

As he started to walk away, Jack asked, "I just remembered, Aimee. Your customers came in this morning for the rings. Did they like them?"

If he thought she looked happy before, she was beaming now. "They loved them! The groom said I helped make this the best elopement ever and that he would tell everyone he knew that they had to come to me for their custom wedding rings." She held her fingers in the air to make air quotes for *everyone*.

At dinner, Andy patted Jack on the back. "I still can't believe that you got those photos of the bald eagles, bro!"

"I know. It's like one of those shots that goes viral. You know the pictures—bald eagles everywhere on a tree, only this time they were covering the beach. It looked like a bald eagle convention."

Aimee grinned. "And then they took flight. Please tell me that you got a lot of photos as they did that."

Jack laughed. "So many. I would say too many, but I'm going to be selling those photos for the rest of my days. They're gorgeous. I can't wait to get home and go through them on the computer."

Aimee's phone rang. She pulled it out of her purse and said, "Grandma. She must be checking on us." She went to the entrance to talk where it was quieter.

Andy said, "It didn't look like you had an office set up in your place, bro. I didn't even notice your computer when I was there."

"I keep putting it away because there isn't a good space to leave it out. But I think I'll have a good spot for it on the table at my new place."

Andy gave him a puzzled expression. "New place? You forgot to mention that."

Molly asked, "I know Mom's renting you one of her places week-to-week. Did you find something permanent?"

Jack glanced over at Aimee. Should he say anything? Then he realized that everyone would find out sooner or later. His brothers would want to visit him once he was in his permanent home. "Aimee's grandfather offered me a cabin on their property." To make it sound more like it was just a business endeavor and not anything personal, Jack quickly added, "They used to rent cabins to people, and they'd fixed this one up for Aimee, but she's happily living in the house with them. They gave me a deal I couldn't refuse." Jack gave what he hoped was a confident smile.

Molly and Andy stared at him.

Then his brother chuckled. "Please tell me you aren't that naïve."

"I agree," Molly said. "Her grandparents must really like you and your prospects as their new grandson."

Jack could feel his face growing hot. "I'm just going to pretend that they didn't think that. Have you seen that cabin, Molly?"

"I have. It's nice. I told Aimee that she should move in there, but she wouldn't listen to me."

Jack said, "Andy, it has the most amazing view of the bay. It's been newly remodeled in colors I can live with. And did I mention that it has an amazing view of the bay?"

Andy laughed. "Okay, I get it. It has a great view. It also has Aimee living next door with two matchmaking relatives. Are you sure you want to go there?"

Jack thought over all the other places that he'd viewed. "It's the best thing I saw, especially at this price. Don't worry.

I'm going to keep my distance from them in the future. I won't go over to dinner very often, even though they've offered."

Molly's and Andy's eyes grew wide. Molly didn't say anything, apparently deciding to stay quiet.

His brother had no such qualms. He started laughing. "How many times have you been to dinner there already?"

"Just twice. But one of those was after I drove Aimee home when she fell asleep as she was trying to close her shop after working too many hours."

His brother waffled his head back and forth. "That's understandable. What about the second night?"

"They asked. Aimee's grandmother is a cook equal to Mom. Would you have turned that down and gone home to eat a sandwich?"

Andy grinned. "I wouldn't have made a sandwich. Remember, I'm the one brother who is actually a decent cook."

"That's probably because you're the baby and Mom didn't get a girl, so she had to teach somebody to cook."

"I like to think that it's because I'm the only one of the five of us who had the talent. Besides, many men are great cooks."

Aimee returned and sat down. "Did I miss anything?"

"Just brothers being brothers." Molly rolled her eyes and pointed at him and Andy. "I'll be the moderator here." To Aimee, she said, "Jack mentioned your grandmother's cooking." Turning to Andy, she added, "I have to vouch for what Jack is saying. Mrs. Jones is some kind of cook. My mouth waters even thinking about her chicken and dumplings."

"I haven't had those. Maybe I can restrain myself about

stopping by too often and just ask when she's going to make those next."

Molly grinned. "If you ask for those saying that you'll come the next time she makes them, my guess is that she'll make them that day."

"She would. She loves taking care of people." Aimee took a sip of her water.

He had a feeling that was true. And she'd do whatever it took to get him to date Aimee. He'd have to keep his distance from both grandparents and their granddaughter.

Jack awoke to the scent of breakfast being made. This was one of the perks of having Andy stay over: he wouldn't let his brothers cook. He rolled out of bed and trudged out into the living area. "Quite a way of waking a guy up. Instead of banging around like any other decent brother would, you just let delicious scents tempt me out of bed."

"And it worked, didn't it?"

Jack laughed. "I don't know what you found to make in my meager supply of food."

"There were a dozen eggs. You don't cook, so I don't know why you bought them."

"I guess I dream of making a decent meal."

Andy laughed. "I've tasted your cooking. Buy frozen pre-made meals. For our breakfast, I found seasonings in the cupboard, which the owners must leave for their guests to use, but you probably hadn't. I put together an omelet with some herbs in it. And I made coffee. And next time I come, I'm bringing food."

"Good plan. I do enjoy a big breakfast."

"You're paying for half of the food bill when I do."

Jack chuckled. "I'll pay for all of it if I get to eat well."

"What's the kitchen like in that place you're renting that's next door to a woman you're crazy about but won't pursue?"

Jack stared at his brother before answering. "That was the most loaded question I've ever heard in my entire life. I think I'll just pick one little piece out of it and tell you that the kitchen in the cabin is similar to this one, only newly remodeled."

"Nice. Then I definitely want to visit. It doesn't have a bed for me there, though, does it?"

"There's a sofa. Mr. Jones didn't mention anything about it being able to fold out to a bed, but if not, I'll get one so you or one our other brothers could stay. Aimee's grandparents can store the one they bought for her in one of the other cabins."

"You like my cooking that much?"

Jack went over and filled up a mug of coffee and looked in on what his brother was making. "It's not that your food is the best food I've ever had—not that it isn't amazing—it's that mine is so bad in comparison." It surprised him that food cooked in this kitchen could turn out good. Sitting, he waited for breakfast.

Andy grinned. "I can definitely vouch for that. I remember that time that Mom and Dad were gone, and we all took turns cooking. I don't even remember what you made—"

"Shrimp and grits. Shrimp were easy to come by in Juneau. I thought, how hard can this be? It's like shrimp over hot cereal."

"But it wasn't good."

"I know, I know. I've always liked meat well done, so I

thought if I cook the shrimp twice as long as the recipe said, then they would be even better. And somehow, the grits came out in a block that I was able to slice off instead of spoon out."

"I'm just glad that we were able to get to the burger place before it closed."

Andy portioned up the omelet and brought it over to the table as Jack held his fork in his hand ready to go.

He took a bite of it as Andy sat down. "Mmm. This is so good. Are you heading back home after breakfast?"

"I've decided that I want to see this new home of yours. My cats have food to last until this afternoon, so I'll help you move this morning. You're coming to lunch at Mom and Dad's tomorrow, right? It's strange to have it on any day but Saturday."

"I missed the last lunch and promised to be there. I guess I'll need to catch everybody up on what's going on here. I know that Dad will want to see the photos I took yesterday."

A short time later, they had showered and shaved and headed out the door with Jack driving in front and Andy following behind in his pickup. Jack got out of the SUV, walked around to the front door, and right on cue, it opened.

Mrs. Jones said, "Drive around to the back. There's a gravel parking pad back there that's a little overgrown but still exists under the grass. That way, you can park closer to your home, and you don't have to walk through the lawn every time. I'll meet you in front of the cabin in a few minutes."

Jack thanked her and then went back to his SUV, stopping Andy, who was opening his door. They drove around to the back, and Jack could see the gravel through some grass. It was set back far enough that he wasn't in the Jones's backyard—he was almost behind it—and he was grateful for that. Andy parked beside him and got out of his truck.

"Aimee's grandmother is waiting by the cabin." Jack took a couple steps and stopped. "I hope I made the right choice in choosing this place."

"Me too, bro. You are in such a tangled up mess with this. If I were interested in the woman, I would not even consider being here."

They continued on. The problem with all of this was that Jack *was* interested in the woman. More than a little bit. Their lives were just headed in different directions. To him, their paths were as different as they would be with one person who wanted to be a farmer and one who dreamed of being a colonist on Mars.

He found both Aimee's grandmother and grandfather at the cabin. Fortunately, Aimee would be at work right now, so she wasn't joining the party.

Her grandfather greeted him. "Good to see you, my boy. And this is?"

"My brother Andy."

"Nice to meet you." The men shook hands, then Mr. Jones said, "Aimee gave us a quick rundown on everywhere she took you yesterday. Was it a good trip?"

"Better than I could have ever imagined. Thank you for allowing her to take me out on the boat."

The man unlocked the door and pushed it open wide. He then gestured for Jack and Andy to enter, and he and his wife followed.

When Andy saw the interior of the cabin, he gave a long, low whistle. "This is very nice."

Jack stepped over to the living room window and motioned Andy over. "Here is the best part."

When Andy stood next to him, he said, "This is an amazing find!"

Mr. Jones joined them at the window. "We've always thought so. It has the same view as the house, and there isn't a finer view anywhere along the road."

Mrs. Jones stood in the kitchen. "We had this fixed up for our granddaughter, so everything you need should be here. There are two sets of sheets, dishes, and pots and pans; there's even toilet paper and tissue in the linen closet in the bathroom."

Andy looked at Jack and raised his eyebrows. He didn't say it, but Jack once again felt like he'd fallen down the rabbit hole. This place was nothing short of amazing.

"It's wonderful, thank you. I'll just run the laundry into town."

"Nonsense." Mrs. Jones said. "You can use our washer and dryer. Just make that one of the nights that you come over for dinner. Throw it in, and then it'll all be ready by the time we're done with dessert. How does that sound?"

He hurried to answer. "Thank you very much. Would you like me to write you a check right now?"

"I'm sure you and Andy will be doing things together today. Can you come to dinner tomorrow? You could bring it then."

Andy helped him out. "We're both going to go up to our parents' house for lunch in Kenai. That would probably mean we'd be back too late for dinner, wouldn't it, Jack?"

Jack was relieved that he didn't have to come up with an excuse for not having yet one more meal with Aimee and her family so soon after the last one. Well, with Aimee. He certainly didn't have any complaints about any of these people. He just didn't want to mislead her.

"Now that I think about it, that would be pushing it. But thank you."

Aimee's grandmother smiled at him and left.

Mr. Jones clapped him on the shoulder. "She's a force to be reckoned with. Just like her granddaughter." He gave a wink and then left.

When Andy had closed the door, he turned to Jack and grinned. "This is an amazing place to live. I take back everything I said about not living next to Aimee."

"With that separate parking area, I think I can avoid contact with her, and it won't be any different than someone living down the hall in an apartment building."

"You're right except for one thing."

Jack looked at his brother. Andy might be the youngest, but he did come up with bits of wisdom. "And what would that be?"

"Two grandparents are trying to pull you two together, and one of them is a grandmother who has figured out that she can get you to do almost anything for a homemade meal." He grinned.

Jack laughed. "There is an unfortunate abundance of truth in that. But I'm going to find a way to be busy whenever she asks. Honestly busy. I'm going to need a new place to go at dinnertime. Maybe I'll just photograph sunsets off the spit every evening for a couple weeks until they get used to that pattern and don't notice when I'm actually here."

"It isn't a bad plan. As long as the weather cooperates." Andy went into the kitchen and started opening up cupboards. Then he opened the fridge and leaned down to look inside. "Wow. They stocked the cupboards and fridge for you. And this isn't food they bought for Aimee." He took out some bread and checked the date on the tag. "This is fresh."

"These must be some of the nicest people that I have ever met in my entire life. I am happy to call them my landlords."

Andy set the bread on the counter and then added some lunchmeat and other things to a stack beside it.

"They even thought of condiments." He took out a jar of pickles and some mustard and mayo. "I'm going to throw together a sandwich to eat on the way back. Do you want me to make one for you too?"

"Why not. And I'll include something extra in the check to cover the food. Remember to give me a list of whatever you want before you come to town next time. I want to make sure that you can cook to your heart's delight."

"As long as you get to eat it."

Jack grinned. "Of course."

As Andy made the sandwiches, he grew silent, then he said, "I know you've told me that there's no way this can work with Aimee. But I like her, and you seem good together."

"No more talk about Aimee. What about Molly?"

"Molly's attractive, and I like her as a person, but it's not going to go anywhere. It's up to you to find someone for her in Homer. Because you're so good with romance, aren't you?" Andy turned toward him and raised an eyebrow.

"Maybe I'll have more success with someone else."

His brother shrugged and started wrapping up the sandwiches. "Well, I'm on my way. I'll see you tomorrow at Mom and Dad's. I hope you enjoy your dinner alone tonight," he said as he picked up the lunch he'd made for himself. With that comment, he went out the door and closed it behind him.

CHAPTER FOURTEEN

*A*imee watched another happy customer go out the door. She missed having Jack here for more than one reason. He made her smile. He also made her workload tolerable. She carried the new job to the back to add to her box. It was only a ring sizing, but there were jobs ahead of it. The simple jobs took a fair amount of time, but they didn't bring in enough money to make a huge difference to her bottom line. As she dropped it in the box, the bell chimed. Sighing, she turned around and went right back out.

"Are you Aimee Jones?" A young woman practically bounced on the tips of her toes as she asked the question, and the man beside her patiently waited.

Aimee cautiously said, "Yes, I am," as she stepped behind the counter to put space between them. The woman looked like she could get a little too exuberant for Aimee's tastes.

The young woman squealed. "We saw the rings that you made for Ethan and Sherry. They're gorgeous. We'd like a set too."

"I can't do another set exactly like that one."

The woman stepped up closer to the counter. "Oh, I don't want ones exactly like that. I have an idea in mind, but I want you to make it."

A warm feeling washed over Aimee. This was what she lived for, the creative work. "Let me grab my sketchpad, and we can start to work on it. You aren't getting married soon, are you?"

The woman bounced a few more times. "No, we're getting married in six months in a big wedding. I would like an engagement ring before then, though, if you could do that?"

Aimee gave a firm nod. She needed to take control of the situation. "Yes, I can. Let's figure out what you want. Then I can let you know how long it will be before I can make that for you. Does that sound okay?"

The woman bounced a couple more times, then reached out and held the hand of the man patiently standing still at her side. "Perfect."

Aimee sketched a design, and they tweaked it, finally coming to a finished idea that in no way resembled what she had made for the other couple. Swirls of white gold with tiny diamonds scattered randomly in the swirls created a design almost the opposite of the other set. It was pretty, light, and feminine, a ring she would like herself. For the man, she created a wedding ring that was diamond-cut in a complementary pattern. She would etch the design all the way around the ring, and the swirls would be attractive but not pretty.

She looked up at the woman and turned the design so that it faced her. The customer bounced, clutched her hands to her chest, and sighed. "Oh, my goodness! That's it. You saw into my head and created exactly what I want." She wiped a tear from the corner of her eye. "This is wonderful, isn't it, Eric?"

He stared at the design. "It's exactly what you said you wanted, but even better because she added things that you and I couldn't even imagine."

"Exactly."

Aimee told him what the rings would cost and accepted their deposit so that she could begin working on them. As soon as she finished up all of her other little projects, but she didn't tell them that. After they left, she went into the back, smiling all the way. She glanced at the desk beside her and could picture Jack sitting there working. And she realized that he must be moved into the cabin on her grandparents' property already. Next door.

Sighing, she sat down to work. It wasn't too much longer before the bell chimed again. Groaning, she pushed back from her desk and trudged toward the doorway, standing straight and putting on her brightest smile. Instead of a customer, it was Molly. A genuine smile crossed Aimee's face.

"I'm so glad to see you!" She looked down at her friend's hands. "And I see you come bearing gifts."

"More like a peace offering." Her friend said the words hesitantly, and Aimee wondered what was coming next. "I need to talk to you about Jack."

Aimee's heart beat faster just at the mention of his name. She didn't say anything, though. She waited for Molly to get rolling. When her friend started on something, it was hard to stop her.

"The two of you are perfect together. You know that, right?"

Molly sat a box of baked goods on the counter, cups of coffee next to it, and gave Aimee a firm stare. "Don't give me any of this garbage about going different directions. Tell me what you think of the man, and don't tell me that you don't care. I won't buy that."

Aimee rubbed her hand over her face. "I don't think I'm sure about how I feel. I like him. He's nice. Sometimes it feels . . . right when he's with me. What does that all add up to?" She shrugged. She felt a tug on her heart as she thought about the two of them together.

"I don't know. I haven't been there myself, but it sounds a whole lot like love to me."

Aimee gave a harsh laugh. "I don't think so. Besides, he's made it quite clear that we do not make a good couple."

"Then you're just going to have to change the man's mind. You do want him for your own, don't you?"

Aimee thought of how wonderful it felt to see Jack smile and to have him beside her, and how her heart had melted when he'd held her hand. Did she want him for her very own?

"You're overanalyzing this."

"That is a distinct possibility, since I have a tendency to do that."

"This is easy. Picture your life *with* him and picture your life *without* him."

Aimee gasped and put her hand over her mouth. "I need him in my life, Molly. He doesn't want me in his life, though. This isn't going to work. I'll just end up brokenhearted."

Her friend sadly shook her head. "Aimee, I think you're going to end up brokenhearted if you *don't* go after him."

"But what do I do? He doesn't want me."

"Then you're just going to have to change his mind." Her friend opened up the box of treats and held it in front of her. "Here. Some fuel to get you going."

CHAPTER FIFTEEN

*A*imee counted the minutes until she could get out of her store and talk to Jack. But how would she do that? He lived next door, but she couldn't just knock on his door anytime she wanted.

When she walked in the door of her grandparents' home, she found Jack sitting in the living room with her grandparents, laughing and talking.

Her grandfather waved her over. "Aimee, come join us. Young Jack here was just telling us about some of the places where he's taken photos here in Alaska."

Aimee stopped at the door. Instead of her having to seek Jack out, here he was in her own home, which unsettled her just a bit. And that had to be the most ridiculous thing she had ever thought in her life.

He kept his eyes on her as she walked into the living room. She gave a small and a completely awkward wave. "Hello, everyone. What did I miss?"

Her grandmother said, "Tell us another story, Jack."

145

Jack didn't say anything but continued to stare at her. He pulled his gaze off of her and looked at her grandparents.

Her grandmother had a knowing smile.

He cleared his throat. "Let me think. I was once in the Brooks Range on a photo-taking trip. A friend offered to fly us out in his floatplane for a couple of days of camping in the far north, so I decided to close the store for a Monday and go. We pitched a tent, and I took photos that afternoon. When we stepped out of our tent the next morning, we discovered that clouds had dropped low, so low that he couldn't take off." His brow furrowed as he told his tale. "We'd thankfully packed extra food in case of a problem because we were there three extra days."

Aimee had sat in her usual chair while he spoke. "What happened to your jewelry store while you were gone?"

Frowning, he looked at her. "Nothing. It was closed *all that time*. I just planned to take a Monday off because Mondays are my slowest days. *Were* my slowest days. Instead, I was closed most of the week, and I had some angry customers who had wanted to pick up jewelry jobs."

A less than happy environment settled over the room.

True to form, her grandfather broke things up. "Don't tell me that you missed the opportunity to take photos while you were there."

Jack swiveled around to face her grandfather, and she could tell it was a struggle for him to focus back on that part of the conversation, but he did.

"No, sir." He started to smile. "The second day, when I stepped out of my tent, I saw a herd of migrating caribou. Hundreds of them. I hiked into the herd and shot photos of them for hours. The photos I got that weekend gave me the income and the courage to sell my jewelry store."

Her grandmother shifted in her chair. This conversation had clearly not gone where they had hoped it would. Jack once again looked unhappy as he thought about the past and his jewelry store.

Her grandmother stood. "Dinner is ready. I was just letting the meat rest while we waited for our Aimee to come home."

They moved into the formal dining room.

Aimee stopped. "Grandma, what are we doing eating in here?"

"Aimee, Jack is company. This is normally where company eats."

Jack held up one hand. "I'm not company, ma'am. Think of me as a friend and your tenant."

"Nonsense. Did you bring your computer, as Carson asked?"

Aimee turned toward Jack. "Computer? Are you helping them with something?" She turned back toward her grandparents. "If you need anything done on the computer, I can help you at any time."

Jack answered. "When I dropped off the rent check, your grandfather insisted I come for dinner and bring my computer so I could show them the photos I took yesterday."

Aimee smiled for the first time since she'd stepped through the door. "Then let's eat. I'm looking forward to seeing some of those. That moment that we stopped at Gull Island and the clouds parted for you? That was a wow." She turned toward her grandparents. "You should have been there. But the good news is, it'll be almost like you were there because of all the photos."

Her grandmother hurried off to the kitchen and returned with a plate of what looked like pork chops—probably her famous recipe that they all loved—a wild rice pilaf, and roasted vegetables. Grandma had gone all out for Jack. Aimee knew that each of these dishes was a favorite recipe.

As they sat, she tried to conjure up an image of eating with Jack at the kitchen table the night he brought her home. As it became clearer, she remembered that he'd been seated next to her. This time, her grandmother hadn't been quite as aggressive in her matchmaking because she did put one person at each of the four sides of the table. Of course, she and Jack were facing each other, but again not a surprise.

Maybe they weren't matchmaking. Maybe they just wanted to be nice to their new tenant. That wouldn't be surprising in the slightest for her grandparents. She'd watched her grandfather put together a box of groceries and leave it on a doorstep when he knew someone was out of work. They were just good people.

At the end of dinner, her grandmother brought her grandfather's favorite dessert out, a chocolate pie. She'd made the perfect end to a fabulous dinner, and Aimee told her grandmother that as they ate the pie.

"Thank you, my dear. I've always enjoyed this particular meal."

Jack sighed as he reached for another bite of the pie. "I second that. Don't tell my mother, but you're in strong competition for best cook on the Kenai Peninsula."

Her grandmother giggled. Giggled! Aimee hadn't known she was capable of that. A compliment from a handsome young man would do that for her personally, and it certainly had worked on an older woman as well.

As soon as they'd finished eating, her grandmother stood to clear the table. She started to refuse Aimee's help, saying, "Stay here with your young man—"

Aimee grabbed some plates and hurried into the kitchen before her grandmother could finish what she'd started to say.

Once they'd cleared the table, they crowded around Jack as he opened his computer and booted it up. As soon as the photos appeared on the screen, everyone leaned in closer to look.

Her grandmother said, "Aimee, why don't you pull a chair right up next to Jack. Then you can see the screen more easily and tell us where you were when he took the photo." She looked up at her husband. "Carson, doesn't that make sense?"

He looked at his wife and gave a nod. "Excellent idea, my dear."

Her grandfather slid a chair beside Jack's, so close that they'd probably be touching. He looked at her like a deer caught in the headlights, but he was also too nice to say anything.

Aimee started to tell them she'd rather stand . . . but nothing would be gained. As she sat, she could feel Jack's warmth through her sweater.

He flipped through the photos. Every time he moved his arm, he brushed against her. She shared the photo's location, and he followed with his thoughts as he'd taken the shot. She caught herself leaning closer to him as he spoke, but she pulled herself away and sat stiffly upright.

When they stopped on one with birds in the air and the sun overhead, she pointed to it and said, "Jack, that is a fabulous photo! How are you selling your photos?"

He paused and turned to her. That meant their faces were much too close. "I sell them through a stock photo site and have sold quite a few to magazines."

"No website?"

He groaned. "Not yet. Andy keeps telling me I need a website. He must have offered a dozen times, maybe more, to build one for me."

"Andy builds websites?"

"Andy is considered somewhat of a genius with websites, enough so that he is able to work at home and take whatever jobs he wants."

Aimee tapped her chin. "When I bought photos online, I found some of Homer but would have loved to have more to choose from. E-commerce would be a good way for you to make more income. Just don't overcharge. I've also been on sites where the photos cost so much money that I have to look elsewhere."

"Why did you need photos of Homer?"

"I wanted the walls of my store to show the town and all its beauty. Those photos were bought from local photographers, some of them online."

Jack said, "I assumed you had taken the pictures."

Her grandfather gave a low chuckle. "Our Aimee is a very skilled jeweler. She's also an excellent boat captain. Please, and I say this with all sincerity, please do not ever hand her a camera and ask her to take a photo."

Jack turned toward Aimee and grinned. "Not good?"

"*So* not good."

Her grandmother laughed. "Remember the photo that you took of your London roommate's cat?"

Aimee leaned forward and rested her head on her fingertips. She sighed and said, "I still don't know how I managed to cut off her head and all of her legs. All that was left was the middle of her body. I know I framed that photo well."

Jack leaned back and roared with laughter. "Okay, so you

can make jewelry for me, and you can take me out in the boat. But you can't take pictures. Is there anything else that you can't do? I want to make sure I never ask for that."

Her grandmother said, "Cooking."

"Also not good?"

"I have tried to teach Aimee to cook a hundred times, probably more. We start with the same ingredients and the same directions, but we sure don't end up with the same product."

"Okay, note to self, never let Aimee cook something for me. That's a problem, though, because if we were ever in a situation where we were alone and there was a stove, I couldn't cook either."

She grinned at him. He'd just painted a very domestic picture. She glanced up at her grandparents, and both of them wore satisfied smiles.

Her grandmother turned to her grandfather and said, "Carson, would you help me with the dishes?"

He looked startled. Aimee didn't remember her grandfather once helping her grandmother with the dishes. After a moment of hesitation, he said, "Of course. Let's go." And before she knew it, her grandparents were gone, and she and Jack were sitting side by side alone.

Jack turned toward Aimee. "What just happened? Was it something I said?"

She stared him in the eyes. "Yes, it was."

"We talked about photos and cooking." His eyes grew wide as he seemed to realize what he'd done. "I didn't mean anything personal by that."

"I know you didn't." But each time they were together, she walked away wishing that he did see her that way.

He fidgeted in his seat and stared at the table. "Dinner was great."

Jack clearly felt trapped. To diffuse the moment, she asked, "Do you alter the images at all? Or are they exactly as you have taken them?"

He stared at his computer screen. "It's a mixture. But just as I would have played with the color a little bit using film—because I did start learning photography with film—I sometimes do little tweaks so it's the best it can be. I don't change a pink sunset into purple or something like that, though. Alaska's natural beauty doesn't need major enhancements."

She put her hand on his arm as he was flipping through the photos. "That one there." She pointed to one of the photos of the otters. "The otters themselves are wonderful and absolutely adorable, but there's a piece of debris floating by and distracting. Can you remove something like that?"

He brought up his photo editing program, imported that photo, and eliminated the debris.

"And the photo is overall just a tiny bit dark. It must have been when the sun went behind the clouds for a while."

He lightened it and turned toward her. "Good eye. This is the kind of editing I like to do. I didn't change the photo; I just made the photo better."

"Jack, I have a high school friend in Anchorage who works for a bank. They're remodeling and redecorating. She mentioned that they're using Alaskan art, so I think you should submit this to them. I suspect you would earn more that way than you would on one of the stock photo sites."

He looked from Aimee to the photo and studied it. "I'll send it in whenever you get me the email address."

She took out her phone and brought it up, showing it to him. She watched him type a short email. He said he was a landscape photographer based out of Homer, had taken the photo the day before, and understood they were searching for original Alaskan art. If this one didn't suit their plans, he had others he could suggest.

"Thank you." He smiled at her, and her heart flip-flopped.

Without thinking, she said, "We do make a good team, don't we?" She bit her lip. "I didn't mean that how it sounded."

He eyed her. She wasn't sure what to make of his speculative glance. Then he suddenly pushed back from his chair, stood, and grabbed his computer, closing it as he walked out of the room. "It's time for me to go home. The good thing is that it's a short walk."

She followed him to the door. "Good night, Jack."

Her grandmother peered out from the kitchen. "See the young man home, Aimee."

Aimee felt her face turning hot. "Grandma!" she hissed.

"It's the polite thing to do," her grandmother said with emphasis, then stepped back in the kitchen like she knew it was going to be done.

Aimee looked up at Jack. "I'm sorry."

He whispered, "I don't mind if you walk me home. I don't want to get lost in the dark, do I?"

She laughed and followed him out. It had grown dark, but the outdoor light illuminated the stone pathway most of the way.

In front of his cabin, he set the computer down on the bench. Then he turned to her. "Aimee, sometimes you seem to be my other half, and I'm sure that we belong together." He took a step closer to her and slid his arms around her waist. "I should not be doing this."

Just as she wondered what 'this' was, but hoping he

intended to kiss her, he lowered his head toward hers. When the light kiss deepened, she wrapped her arms around him. He gently cupped the back of her head with his hand.

Too quickly, he stepped back. "I'm so sorry. I never should have done that. This can't work out."

Her chest tightened, and she struggled to speak. "Why can't it, Jack?"

"I feel chains tightening around me."

She shook her head. "Chains? Is that how you see a relationship?"

"No. It's your jewelry store. You don't understand how much stress it caused me to own my jewelry store. I ended up having to see a counselor toward the end. I desperately wanted to make a business out of my photography, and I was doing well with it. I had it in local galleries, but I didn't have time to nurture that business when the jewelry store was taking everything I had." He took another step back. "Getting close to you makes me feel trapped in a retail business again. Your chains would be mine." He dropped to the bench. "I'll move out of here if you want me to."

How could things go from normal to wonderful to terrible in minutes? She swallowed hard. "You don't need to do that, Jack. If I have my way about it, we'll never see each other again." She turned on her heels and raced back to the house.

Jack watched Aimee go. In a short amount of time, she'd come to mean a lot to him. But how could he live with her business? He put his key in the lock and stepped inside his new home, the joy of finding a permanent place dimmed by what had just happened. He set the computer down on the table, sat on the couch, and leaned forward, resting his forehead on his hands. Then he looked heavenward. "What am I going to do?" When no answer came, he trudged off to bed, hoping that life would make more sense the next day.

As he stared into the mirror the next morning before he shaved, he knew two things. One: Aimee was special. Two: he needed his family. He was glad that today was the weekly lunch, that he was able to go to his parents' house and see his brothers.

As he drove the hour and a half or so to Kenai, he kept thinking over the last week, wondering what he could have done differently. His only conclusion was that he should have kept walking the first time he'd noticed the messed-up display in the jewelry store's window.

He'd been in there twice before, had known he'd been set up, but he'd remained untouched. Bree may have started this, but he'd returned on his own. He knew Bree had hoped that she'd made a match and in the end she almost had. If only she'd chosen someone like Molly, who had a bakery. But he knew Molly wasn't his special someone.

Aimee watched the sun rise over Kachemak Bay from her rocking chair on the front porch. Hours of lying in bed had resulted in two things: zero sleep and a sore elbow because she'd tossed and turned so violently that she'd hit it on her nightstand.

The view helped. She'd come home to Homer for family. But the view soothed her soul.

When the sun was high in the sky, she rested her head

against the back of the chair and tried to relax. Footsteps sounded on the gravel path to her left. Had Jack thought over his words and returned to say he'd been wrong?

The footsteps paused for a moment, and her heart beat faster. Then they moved hurriedly away, and she heard a vehicle start. Seconds later, Jack's SUV went down the driveway and out of sight up the road.

He'd left.

CHAPTER SIXTEEN

*W*hen Jack arrived at his parents' house, he was relieved to see Andy getting out of his truck. He needed to talk to his brothers. Adam pulled up as Jack walked up the steps to the house, alone this time, his wife and girls elsewhere. Other cars told Jack that Mark and Noah were probably here as well. He wondered if they'd brought their fiancées.

He opened the door to the usual cacophony of sounds. As he started through the doorway, Adam's dog Emma squeezed beside him into the house to get to her friend, who bounded over. The two of them raced down the hallway, turned, and came back toward the living room. Experience had taught Jack to stay in the doorway and out of the way.

Noah yelled, "Zeke, halt!"

The dog ground to a stop. Noah pointed toward the back door, which Zeke happily trotted over to along with Emma. With the dogs in the backyard, Jack went further into the house.

Andy grinned. "You made it, bro. I wasn't sure that you would with that pretty lady you have down in Homer."

Jack did his best to pretend everything was okay. "I told you she was just a friend." He smiled and hoped it looked genuine.

Andy frowned and gave him a look that said he hadn't believed it for a second. No one asked anything else about Aimee through the meal. Being around his family helped unwind the pain around his heart. But every time he started to relax, he'd remember something Aimee had said or done.

When they finished dinner, Adam spoke up. He put his hand on his stomach and rubbed it. "I think I could use a break between your wonderful lunch, Mom, and whatever you have for dessert." He stood. "Let's go outside, men, and get some fresh air with the dogs for a few minutes."

Andy put his hand on his father's shoulder and gave a slight shake of his head as he went by. Only the five brothers would be going outside. Jack had been part of an intervention with Noah to make him see the light about Rachel a couple of months ago. He wondered who was on the hot seat tonight because it looked like another one of those. He was relieved to know that it would have nothing to do with him. Andy was the only one who even had a clue that he'd spent a lot of time with Aimee. He'd told Adam about stopping by again, but nothing beyond that. He was safe.

When the door closed behind them, the dogs raced over to see their owners and check out all of the other humans who had stepped into their domain. Then they bounded away again and raced around the yard.

Adam said, "I've asked you all to be here because Jack needs our help."

Jack spun around to look at his older brother and pointed at his own chest. "What do *I* need help with?" He really hoped this had nothing to do with Aimee because he wasn't ready to talk to anyone about that and maybe never would be. He just wanted it to go away forever.

Adam sighed. "It has come to my attention—"

Jack turned to Andy and raised an eyebrow. His brother shrugged to say he was sorry, but it needed to be done.

"—that he's gotten himself tangled up in a confusing romance. Does that about sum it up, Jack?"

Jack thought through those words. "That's a good way to put it. Except that I resolved it last night. I told her that we wouldn't make a good couple because of her jewelry store."

His brothers look startled.

"Why did you do that?" Adam asked

"It was a bad match all along, Adam. I know that Holly is your wife, and her sister Bree started all of this, but Aimee owns a jewelry store." He said the last words with emphasis, knowing that everyone would be able to understand what that meant to him.

But they didn't seem to. "I know you owned a jewelry store, Jack," Mark said. "But what does that have to do with anything?"

"It matters because she's tied to a jewelry business. It's a six-day-a-week, no vacation, can-barely-take-a-day-off business. I just sold one of those. I can't tell you the sense of relief I felt the moment it belonged to someone else. Why would I want to sign up for more time with that?"

"Because you love her?" Adam almost shouted the words at him. "Isn't that enough of a reason?"

Jack glanced around at the faces of his brothers. "Doesn't

anyone understand what it was like for me with that business?"

Adam put his hand on Jack's arm. "Jack, we understand what it was like when *you* owned the jewelry store, but this isn't your store. It belongs to Aimee. Doesn't that make it different?"

Did it? No. "If I ever have someone to share my life with, I'd like for it to be someone who could travel with me. Maybe not all the time, but a jewelry store in a tourist town will be busy in the summer, the same time when I want to take most of my photos in Alaska." He stood with his shoulders back and looked at his brothers one by one. "I know I'm right. This can't work."

As he turned to walk away, Noah, who had been quiet up until that point, said, "You can find a way to make this work, Jack. If she means enough to you."

Noah's quiet voice hurt even more than the other voices. He didn't see any way to make that happen. No matter how much he might want that to be possible.

Driving home, he had a container on the seat next to him with a piece of blueberry pie in it. He hadn't wanted dessert, but his mother wouldn't let him leave without it and a fork in case he got hungry on the way. Traffic slowed to a stop for a few minutes, so he grabbed the fork and took a bite, thinking over the afternoon. He never thought he'd be the object of an intervention by his brothers. His best answer was to forget about Aimee and focus on work.

Traffic opened up, and a few minutes later, he continued on. Driving through Anchor Point, he considered places that he could go to get away for a while, places where he wouldn't have a chance of seeing his neighbor.

Halibut Cove Lagoon came to mind. He knew there were

state cabins there that he could stay in for a small fee. He'd see if there was an opening in one, schedule it, and pay someone to take him across the bay. He'd get out of Aimee's way, take some great photos, and focus again on the work he loved.

CHAPTER SEVENTEEN

*J*ack admired the view from his picnic spot on China Poot Lake. This week, he'd hiked dozens of miles of trail through the park and snapped hundreds of photos.

Alone.

He tried to take in the peacefulness of the lake as he ate his sandwich. A mosquito interrupted his attempt, buzzing near his ear, and he swatted it away. He heard laughter from far off. This time of year, he saw few other hikers and those only at a distance. Some of the trails had been so overgrown with brush that he'd gotten lost multiple times, but he'd kept going.

He took a bite of the peanut butter sandwich. Hiking here meant he'd walked the same trail the group had when Aimee brought them to the lagoon. He'd paused at First Lake on his way here this morning and pictured her being there with him, then he'd hurried further down the trail to this lake.

The boat would return for him tomorrow morning. Should he go home?

Earlier today, he'd thought about calling Aimee, but the night he'd left, he'd said what he needed to say. Besides, he'd turned his phone off and put it in his duffle bag, reserving it only to reschedule his pickup time and for emergencies. Did missing Aimee count as an emergency?

After brushing off his hands, he picked up his lunch bag and stood. He and Aimee weren't a good fit. In fact, he wished Bree had never played matchmaker. He'd call the water taxi and have his pickup delayed another week. His family knew where he was. Andy had even been to Halibut Cove Lagoon, so they shouldn't worry.

Time would pass quickly, and he'd forget about Aimee.

Three days later, Jack ran his fingers through his shaggy hair and watched bald eagles swoop over the water in front of his cabin set high above the lagoon on a rocky hill. He grabbed his camera and raced outside to capture the birds. Standing on the dock, he snapped photos, and a sea otter surfaced and flipped to its back to float by in front of him.

Paradise. He'd booked a reservation in paradise.

But this view needed to be shared with someone. When he returned to Homer, he'd like to stop by Aimee's store and show her the photos. He couldn't do that, though. He'd been clear about ending any possibilities of a relationship with her.

Why hadn't that made him happy?

The problem was that he enjoyed her company. He'd certainly enjoyed kissing her. He wanted to share every part of his life with Aimee. Maybe loving someone meant that you found a way even when there didn't seem to be a way.

"No!" he shouted. He couldn't love her! He took a step back into nothingness. Waving his arms in the air, he flew backward and sat in the lagoon, raising his camera above the water as he splashed down. He jumped to his feet and wiped it off on his still-dry chest.

He couldn't have fallen in love with Aimee. Could he? He tested the words out loud. "I love Aimee Jones." Honesty surrounded them.

Instead of feeling weak saying them, he felt strong. Louder, he said, "I love Aimee." None of the expected panic set in. He'd known they couldn't be together. She had what he couldn't tolerate being around.

Could he love her and stay far away from her?

His wet jeans felt colder when a breeze whipped up on the incoming tide. Hurrying toward his cabin and dry clothing, he considered his options. He'd have to move. Away from Homer. Away from Aimee.

Inside, he threw wood into the stove and lit it. The warmth burst into the room. Standing, he watched the flames for a moment, then closed the door on it. Once he'd changed, he sat in a chair in front of the window, his favorite place here. The view vanished as he pictured Aimee. Spending those days with her in her jewelry store hadn't been unpleasant.

Jewelry stores aren't bad places.

The revelation rocked his world. Only his store had been bad because he hadn't wanted to be there.

He jumped to his feet. He'd been stupid to think anything else! It was time to go home. Digging out his phone, he rehearsed the words he'd use when he saw her again. He'd seen the pain in her eyes that last night. Could she forgive him?

He dialed the water taxi. They said they'd pick him up tomorrow when the tide and their schedule permitted.

Checking the tide chart, he knew that would either be right after dawn or late afternoon.

CHAPTER EIGHTEEN

*A*imee bludgeoned her way through another day. Jack had told her he couldn't have a relationship with her over a week ago. She wasn't sure that she'd slept at all the first night and barely better than that since then. She kept replaying what had happened, wondering if she should have done or said something differently. Jack hadn't returned. She didn't know if he'd moved away permanently or if he'd eventually be back.

She'd done her best to be kind to each of her customers and give them the best service that she possibly could, but she wasn't herself by a mile.

By noon, she was really dragging. She hadn't gotten any new design jobs today, only another ring sizing and a fairly simple repair to a necklace. Everything had seemed exciting when she'd first opened the doors to her business, but as time passed, she wished she could hire someone to take care of the simple jobs so she could focus on what she really loved to do, what she'd spent years learning to do well.

The bell chimed just as she started to solder a setting to

the necklace for Jack's mother. There was no stopping until she finished soldering this. With it done, she dropped it in the pickling solution. Molly came around the corner as she started to push back from the bench.

"What are you doing here? Isn't this your busy time?"

"Check your watch." Molly tapped her left wrist.

Aimee did as she'd said. "Oh, my goodness! It's 3:15 already. I lost time again. And I've been up and down so many times that I still haven't set this stone. I'm going to have to stay late to get work done after the store is closed."

"Since you think it's noon, that must mean you missed lunch. Again."

Aimee frowned. "Yeah. I did. I think I had something for breakfast, though." Had she?

"You *think* you had breakfast?" Molly dragged over the chair from the desk and sat facing her friend. "First, here's lunch for you."

Aimee did her best to smile and look enthusiastic about the food, but she wasn't very hungry. She reached into the bag anyway and pulled out a sandwich. "It's?"

"Veggie on whole wheat. Your favorite."

"Yum." She forced enthusiasm into the word. She didn't feel like talking about everything that had happened with Jack, so she hoped that Molly would believe she'd done her job and leave. Not that she didn't love her friend, but sometimes you just wanted to wallow alone.

Molly continued. "Second, it's obvious something is wrong with you, and you're going to have to talk to me, or I'm not going to leave. I know this has to do with Jack. I've left you alone to give you private time but no more." Molly leaned back in the chair, folded her arms, and stared at Aimee.

Aimee set the untouched lunch to the side. "What gave me away?"

"Are you kidding? I've seen happier expressions on sharks. Do you wish Jack would ask you out? Is that it?"

"He told me that he feels like I'm his other half, that we belong together."

Molly grinned. "That's wonderful! I think you two are great together." She stared at Aimee for a second and then added, "But you're not happy. You don't want him in your life, is that it? And now he's living next door? Oh my, that would be bad, wouldn't it?" She shook her head, making a "tsk-tsk" sound.

Aimee closed her eyes. "No, Molly, I've totally fallen for Jack. But he won't have a relationship with anybody who has a jewelry store."

Molly cocked her head to the side, then she tapped her ear. "I must not have heard you right. He won't date anyone who owns a jewelry store? That doesn't make sense. He owned a jewelry store. I'm right about that, aren't I?"

"Exactly right. And that's why he won't have a relationship with me. He was chained to his store, and he doesn't even want to have anything to do with someone who's chained to a store like this."

"I'm sorry, Aimee. I know you love this business."

Aimee sighed.

"You *do* love this business, don't you?" Molly asked. "It was your dream forever. I remember when we would Skype while you were in London, you told me how you wanted to have a store. And now you do. It's a cute store too."

Aimee stood and paced from one side of the room to the other. "I'm not sure if it's because I'm so depressed about what's been going on with Jack or maybe all the stress of trying to finish that wedding ring set on time, but I feel like I'm drowning in a sea of small jobs that aren't allowing me to do the bigger jobs. And I can't hire anybody due to an abundance of small jobs because they don't pay enough for me to do that. I'm stuck in a loop, and I don't know what to do."

"This reminds me of when I was trying to decide whether or not I wanted to have a restaurant serving breakfast, lunch, and dinner, or a simpler bakery and coffee shop. I finally decided that baking is what brought me joy. Having a place to serve people made that even better for me because I got to watch them enjoy it. So my whole business works." She gave Aimee a hard stare. "Can you just make jewelry? Is that what your mentor did?"

Aimee frowned, pursing her lips as she thought about his business. "He did, but he was also a teacher, so that wasn't his whole income or how he spent all of his time. Besides, the students did a lot of the smaller parts of the jobs, and he did the higher-skilled things while students watched and worked up to that level."

Aimee paced back and forth across the room several times.

Molly reached out and caught her around the wrist. "Stop running. What do you really want? Do you want this store? I hate to see you leave Homer."

"Not going to happen. Homer is my home. That's one thing I know for sure. This is where I want to live and stay. I also know that I want Jack. *And* I want to make jewelry."

"That's three things."

Aimee gave her a mock glare. "So it's three things. But it's three things that don't all fit together."

Molly stood. "Eat your sandwich. You can't think and work if you don't have any fuel. I'll go back to work and clean up for the day." She started to leave, then added, "Remember, call me anytime. I'm here for you."

Aimee ran over and hugged her friend. "Thank you. It means so much to me that someone's on my side."

Molly stepped back and said, "I think there are a lot of people on your side. You just need to figure out what you want."

Aimee watched her friend leave, then she ate her lunch and got back to work. It turned out to be a quiet afternoon, so she was able to get more work done than expected and left on time, feeling grateful for both.

As she drove home, she thought about what she wanted. She needed help with her jewelry store. Or she needed a way that she could only make jewelry, that she wouldn't have to wait on customers and do the repair jobs. She might be able to find someone to buy the store, but where would she do her jewelry work then?

Years ago, before she'd decided to have a storefront, her grandparents had offered to turn one of the cottages into a workshop for her. Could that be the answer?

Still confused when she entered her grandparents' home, she heard more than the voices of her grandmother and grandfather in the kitchen. Going that way, she walked in and found Andy. She hurried over to him. "Did something happen to Jack?"

"Calm down, Aimee. He's okay. Well, he's physically okay."

"Where is he? I haven't seen him in over a week." Ten days to be exact.

Andy looked at her grandparents and then at her. "Is there somewhere we can talk, Aimee?"

Aimee was tired of trying to sort all of this out alone.

"Let's just all talk together. Will that be okay, Andy?"

He shrugged but looked a little uncomfortable. "That's fine with me."

Her grandmother said, "Let's all sit down at the table. Can I get you a cup of coffee, Andy?"

"That would be very nice."

Once they were seated, he turned toward Aimee. "First, I need to know if you're interested in Jack."

"I most definitely am."

"Good. I didn't think I was reading the situation wrong. He's twisted up about the fact that you have a jewelry store. It's kind of irrational, but he hated his store in the end because he could never get away from it."

"I know. He told me that my store felt like chains around him. And I told him I never wanted to see him again."

Her grandmother gasped but remained silent.

"The four of us brothers got together and spoke to him. I'm not sure he listened. I think he might listen to you, though, if you talk to him."

"I can try, but he didn't before. Where is he?"

Andy studied her as though he was making the decision about whether or not to tell a secret. "I think he may be very angry with me for telling you, but all four of us brothers have agreed that this is the right thing to do."

Aimee motioned forward with her hand. "Where is he?"

"He's at Halibut Cove Lagoon in one of the state-owned cabins. He said he needed to get away. We're all kind of worried about him because he's been there for a while. At first, he said that a boat would come back for him in a week, but that if he wasn't ready to come back, he'd tell the captain to return in another week. He didn't come back."

She looked over at her grandfather.

He said, "Take a boat, my dear. This time of year, I don't need them all, so the *Terri Marie* is just sitting there all fueled up and waiting for you."

Aimee jumped to her feet, kissed first her grandfather and then her grandmother, and went around the table to hug Andy. "I'm on my way. I'm in a talk-this-man-out-of-his-stupidity mood!"

Andy laughed. "I knew you were right for him." After a second's pause, he added, "And I wouldn't use the word *stupid* with him right away."

She laughed. "Don't worry."

By the time she'd changed her clothes for the trip and grabbed her coat, her grandmother had a picnic basket ready for her. "The two of you can share a meal and talk it over. I'd like to think that I contributed in some way." Her grandmother reached out and gave her a quick squeeze. "You go after your man, sweetie."

"I will, Grandma. He's going to be your grandson-in-law if it's the last thing I do."

Her grandfather said, "Be careful with my boat. I don't want this to be the last thing you do."

She grinned.

Her grandfather added. "One more thing you've apparently forgotten: I checked the tide table, and you can go into the lagoon, but don't stay too long because it will soon be on its way out."

"Thank you for checking! I'll be careful."

CHAPTER NINETEEN

*A*imee did her best to not break any speed limits on her way down to the harbor. She got the boat going quickly and out onto Kachemak Bay. As she plowed through the water, heading straight for Halibut Cove, she considered the argument she'd had with Jack. He hated her jewelry store. She'd been pretty stressed out about it lately too. She enjoyed crafting jewelry, and it was fun to work with customers on their special project, but that didn't have to be in a retail storefront. Maybe selling the store and having a private workshop somewhere in Homer solved everything.

She headed straight into the cove and then slowed down for the turn into Halibut Cove Lagoon. As she maneuvered the boat slowly through the lagoon and a cabin could be seen on the shore, she remembered that there were multiple cabins and that she didn't know which one was his. The dock came into view along with a man who sat on it holding a camera and pointing it toward the sky. He lowered his camera and turned toward the oncoming boat.

Jack.

When she pulled up alongside the dock, he jumped to his feet. As soon as she turned off the engine, he said, "Aimee?"

She turned toward him hesitantly. What if he'd lost interest in her? He'd been out here a while and had had plenty of time to think, rethink, and overthink the time they'd had together.

He slung his camera strap over his shoulder and hurried over to the boat. His first words to her were, "I'm sorry. Can you ever forgive me? I love you, Aimee Jones. Please get down off that boat and let me hold you close."

Aimee jumped off the boat onto the dock and stepped into Jack's arms. She felt his warmth and—she hoped—his love sink into her, then stepped back. "I have something that I've come to tell you, Jack. I love you. And it's really stupid that you don't want me to have a jewelry store." She felt like adding "so there" but didn't. Then she realized she'd used the word *stupid*.

Instead of being angry with her, he grinned. "I have come to realize that you are absolutely correct. I've been sitting out here all alone, thinking about my future. It was lonely, and it wasn't going to get any better." He dropped to one knee. "I don't have a ring to give you. I think you probably want to make one yourself, anyway, but I'd like to ask you to marry me, Aimee Jones, with your store, grandparents, Homer, and all. Will you do me the honor of becoming my wife at the earliest possible time and place?"

She nodded. "Yes, I will." He stood and wrapped his arms around her, pulling her close. His camera pressed into her side, but she didn't care. If he could take her with a jewelry store, she would be able to take him with all the cameras he could carry.

This time she leaned up and kissed him, pouring all of the

emotion of the last couple of weeks into the kiss. He pulled her tighter and moved his hand to her cheek in a sweet and gentle way.

When they stepped back and looked into each other's eyes, she knew she was seeing her future.

Aimee said, "I have some great news."

"And what would that be? I don't know what on earth could top the news that you're going to marry me."

"I've decided to sell the jewelry store."

Jack took a step back and frowned. "I don't want you to do that for me, Aimee. It's not right for me to steal your dream."

"Jack, my decision is based on the fact that I either need someone to help me or I need to sell the store. My grandparents said years ago that I could work out of one of the small cabins, turn it into a workshop. I wouldn't have a storefront. Maybe I'd be able to meet customers in town at somewhere like Cinnamon's."

He seemed to be weighing his next words. Sighing, he said, "I'd also come to a conclusion about the jewelry store. I realized that when it wasn't mine, it didn't stress me out. Once I'd shoved that trainload of baggage that I brought on our journey to the side, I discovered I didn't mind your jewelry store. Not only that, but doing some of the repair jobs was fine with me, and I didn't mind waiting on the customers. I couldn't do it all the time because I do need to pursue my photography career, but if there were times that you needed some extra help, that would be okay. The one thing I would like, though, is that we could take some vacations together. Could we work that out?"

She grinned. "I'm sure we could. I don't want to be

married to my business anymore. I want my business to work for me."

"That is completely up to you. I'm going to let you choose later whether or not you keep your store. Right now, I only have one request."

She thought through everything they'd said, and it all seemed fairly well covered. "What's that?"

He stepped forward and put his hand on her cheek again. "That you kiss me, and you keep doing that until we have to go back."

She groaned.

"That wasn't the happy sigh that I was looking for."

"Jack, the tide's going out. We need to get out of here now. Can I kiss you in Homer?"

He laughed. "I don't care where we are, Aimee. You have my permission to kiss me now and forever."

Keep reading for the Bonus Epilogue.

20

BONUS EPILOGUE

*N*oah felt that lunch at Mom and Dad's house had gone well—until Adam tapped each of the men on one of their shoulders and motioned for them to go outside. Today all the brothers except Jack had come. Bree's husband Michael and her sister Jemma's husband Nathaniel had joined them. Noah didn't know who in the group was being singled out for a brotherly intervention, but he thought he'd be in the clear. And with temperatures well below freezing, he hoped it would be a short talk.

Adam smiled and said, "Mom and Dad, we're going to throw a ball for the dogs."

Rachel started to rise, but Noah leaned over to his fiancée and said, "Be right back." She nodded in understanding.

The men put on their winter coats and boots and headed into the backyard. When Zeke, Chloe, and Emma raced over to their humans, Adam picked up a ball and threw it, sending the three dogs scrambling to get to it first.

Adam started the conversation. "I'm concerned about Andy."

Jack frowned. "I am too. When Lori broke up with him, Jack dove into work to escape his hurt. But quite a bit of time has passed, and I know he's still putting in eighty-plus hours a week. He finishes building one client's website, then immediately moves on to the next job."

Mark said, "When he helped me build Maddie's house last summer, that was the one time I've seen him relax for more than an hour or two."

Noah added, "He pushes himself hard. I know he picked up the pace again as soon as he got home from Maddie's. I've tried to get him to go out to lunch when I have extra time between flights, but he always gives the same answer: too busy." When his dog Zeke brought him the ball, Noah threw it and the dogs ran after it.

Michael raised his hand. "Can a non-family member comment?"

Adam patted him on the shoulder. "You're married to my wife's sister. You're family."

"Then I'll mention that before I met Bree, I worked more hours than I should. We need a distraction for him, a woman who pulls him away from his work. Does anyone know a special someone for Andy?"

Noah heard man after man say, "No."

Nathaniel's voice held more hope. "I have a client who needs a website in a hurry."

Mark's brow furrowed as he said, "That helps how?"

"She's kind and pretty. And her business is failing because of her current website."

Mark pointed at Jack. "He's the knight in shining armor who rescues damsels in distress."

Adam stepped in. "Andy's had his moments. Remember when he dropped everything to re-do the church website?

And the time he built a website for the animal shelter at no charge?"

"I forgot Andy was an animal lover." Nathaniel grinned. "She's perfect for him."

Adam raised an eyebrow. "Because?"

"She makes and sells dog treats."

Jack shook his head. "You must not remember being at Andy's house. There are cats everywhere, but no dogs. I don't know if he even likes dogs."

Nathaniel winced. "You're right! I'd forgotten about the cats. But they're both animal lovers. That should be helpful, right?"

Adam rubbed his hands on his arms. "If we didn't have to get this settled before we froze to death or Mom came out here to get us, I'd say to dig deeper and find more options."

Mark blew on his hands and stomped his feet to warm them up. "Does everyone agree that she's the one for Andy?"

The men all shrugged.

Noah said, "I guess so. How do we get them to meet?"

Nathaniel said, "I may have the solution. I've sent my marketing clients to Andy for a website in the past. If I can talk him into doing her website, then he'd follow through. Maybe we could figure out a way for them to meet in person later."

Adam shrugged. "He's loyal. He'd do what he said he'd do." He glanced around the group. "Are we in agreement?"

In unison, the group said, "Yes."

Adam said, "Then we're moving ahead with the plan. Get in the house before you freeze." As they turned to go back inside, Adam frowned and added, "This match seems less organized than the ones the women managed. It will be a surprise if it works."

Jack grinned. "Andy always liked surprises."

As they walked toward the door, Noah said, "I can follow up after Nathaniel calls to check in on Andy and mention this woman."

Mark said, "It's wintertime, so I'm not doing as much home construction. I could also call Andy and ask if he's been able to help the woman Nathaniel told us about at lunch."

Adam stomped his feet on the back step to knock the snow off his boots. "*Be subtle.* Andy will run away if he thinks we're playing matchmaker." Adam seemed about to add something when his dog raced over and leaped into his arms. "Are you cold, Emma?" The dog licked his cheek, and Adam carried her inside.

As the men entered the house, Noah whispered to Mark. "I'm not sure if I'm supposed to call him. And I don't know when to do it if I am."

Mark whispered back, "I'm not sure either, except that I know someone needs to follow-up or he may forget about her."

"But should we *both* call?"

"More is better, right?"

Noah was about to argue that it might not be when he heard his mother say dessert was being served. The men hurried back to the dining room.

He'd be surprised if this match went well. But like Andy, Noah liked surprises.

WHAT'S NEXT?

Jack's brother Andy is the last O'Connell brother to meet his match. Both Andy and Samantha have been hurt in the past. When she lands on his doorstep in the middle of the Alaskan winter, Andy has to help. But he doesn't want more than friendship. His cats and her dog might make their problems more challenging. Or maybe they'll be able to help. Get *Surprisingly Matched* to find out!

Matchmakers Jemma, Bree, and Holly met their husbands in the Alaska Dream Romance series. If you haven't read them yet, you don't want to miss *Falling for Alaska* (Jemma's story), *Loving Alaska* (Bree's story), and *Crazy About Alaska*, (Holly and Adam's story).

And there's a FREE, short story tied to these books. Pete and Cathy are in *Falling for Alaska*. Pete—Nathaniel's lawyer —and Cathy—a woman on a hike with Jemma—are minor characters, but their cute first meeting is a FREE short story. I liked them so much that I brought them back in *Crazy About Alaska*. Get your FREE short story at cathrynbrown.-com/together.

ROMANCES BY CATHRYN BROWN

Alaska Dream Romances

Falling for Alaska - Jemma & Nathaniel

Loving Alaska - Bree & Michael

Merrying in Alaska - Leah & Ben

Crazy About Alaska - Holly & Adam

Alaska Matchmakers Romances (Adam's Brothers)

Accidentally Matched - Noah & Rachel

Finally Matched - Mark & Maddie

Hopefully Matched - Jack & Aimee

Surprisingly Matched - Andy & Samantha

Nashville Secrets Romances

How to Marry a Country Music Star

ABOUT CATHRYN

Writing books that are fun and touch your heart

Even though Cathryn Brown always loved to read, she didn't plan to be a writer. She earned two degrees from the University of Alaska, one in journalism/public communications, but didn't become a journalist.

Years passed. Cathryn felt pulled into a writing life, testing her wings with a novel and moving on to articles. She's now an award-winning journalist who has sold hundreds articles to local, national, and regional publications.

The Feather Chase, written as Shannon L. Brown, was her first published book and begins the Crime-Solving Cousins Mystery series. The eight-to-twelve-year-olds in your life will enjoy this contemporary twist on a Nancy Drew–type mystery.

Cathryn enjoys hiking, sometimes while dictating a book. She also unwinds by baking and reading.

Cathryn lives in Nashville, Tennessee, with her professor husband and adorable calico cat.

Made in the USA
Columbia, SC
12 November 2022

71072089R00114